THE DONOR

BRENDA ROTHERT

SILVER SKY PUBLISHING, INC.

CHAPTER ONE

Shelby

IT STARTED WITH A KISS. Or more accurately, with a screaming baby.

An hour ago, I was immersed in a state supreme court opinion on local ordinance enforcement, a Schubert vinyl record serving as the soundtrack for my home office. Soon, though, the only thing I heard was the racket coming through the wall of the apartment above mine. It wasn't just your average crying baby—it was a shrieking, incredibly pissed-off baby.

I told myself to focus. Get in the zone and tune out the noise. I'd somehow gotten through contractors reroofing the neighboring building last fall, hadn't I?

The contractors didn't *wail*, though. I would have preferred an incessant alarm clock to the baby upstairs, and I couldn't say the same for the nonstop hammering. My god, the absolute lung capacity of that child.

Glaring at the ceiling, I yelled, "Enough already!" and started reading a paragraph of the opinion for the fourth time. I'd budgeted *exactly* enough time to finish this job and start my next one on time, but thanks to my new neighbors, I was going to have to work this weekend.

The baby's cries were turning from angry to mournful, and I frowned at my computer screen. What if my new neighbors were trash humans who had abandoned the baby? Clearly someone wasn't taking care of it.

I stood up, scolding myself for waiting an entire hour to go up there. The kid couldn't feed itself, after all. This had to be a problem with the blond twentysomething with a pixie cut I'd seen carrying boxes up the stairs a week ago, or her partner. Whoever it was, they were about to get an earful from me.

Grabbing the keys to my apartment, I walked out the front door, locking it behind me, and stormed up the stairs, stomping my feet on each one to show Blondie how annoying loud neighbors could be.

If she was even there. I pounded on the door of apartment five, vowing to kick it open and go help the baby if no one answered within a minute.

"You've got thirty seconds," I yelled at the closed door. "Then I break it down!"

The door flew open, and Blondie gave me a wild-eyed look, cradling the crying baby in her arms while bouncing up and down gently.

"Break it down?" She looked me up and down. "With what, your hands?"

This bitch. I shook my head.

"*More importantly*," I said sharply, "I work from home. And I can't focus with your kid screaming at the top of its lungs."

I crossed my arms and held her gaze, waiting for her to go on the defensive. Instead, she surprised me, her shoulders sinking.

"She's not my kid, and I don't know shit about babies. My friend had to rush to the hospital because her dad had a heart attack, and she couldn't find a sitter, so…I'm sorry."

An hour of built-up rage drained out of me in an instant.

"Try feeding her," I suggested. "Or changing her."

"I've tried every single thing on Josie's list, and nothing is helping. I fed her, changed her, walked around with her, talked to her…"

"Well, can't you just…rock her or something?" I asked.

"I've rocked her while sitting, while standing, and while walking. I even turned on some Soundgarden and tried rocking while rocking. Nothing."

I rolled my eyes. "You tried to soothe a baby with Soundgarden?"

"I'm desperate. Got any better ideas?"

I frowned at her, because *yes*, I did. "Brahms?"

"Are they on Spotify?"

I was twenty-eight, and ashamed of my generation. Shoving my keys into the pocket of my cardigan, I sighed softly.

"Look, I have some music that might help. Why don't you bring—" I gestured at the infant and Blondie interjected.

"Iris. This is Iris, and I'm Marlowe."

Iris unleashed her fury again, the noise deafening.

"I'm Shelby," I said loudly. "Let's go. Like right now."

My new neighbor nodded. "Come on in while I grab my phone and keys." She stepped aside, allowing me to enter the apartment.

I could only take four steps into the apartment before I was stopped short by boxes. *A lot of boxes.* Had anything been unpacked yet?

"It's still a bit of a mess," she said, waving a hand, shifting the baby to her hip so she could shove her phone in her back pocket and hook a finger into her keys. "But it's only been ten days, so I'll get there eventually."

She walked toward me, Iris aiming for a world record in screaming. "So is it just you in your apartment, or do you have a family?"

I answered quickly. "Just me. How about you?"

She shrugged. "Just me for now. If you see a guy with longish black hair coming in or out of my apartment, please kick me directly in the vagina."

My jaw dropped in shock, then sank even lower when she tried to pass the baby over so she could lock her door.

Hell no. She'd agreed to babysit; I hadn't.

"Let me get that," I said, taking the keys instead of the kid and locking the door for her.

"We broke up like a month ago," she continued, raising her voice so I could hear her over Iris. "Rock won't stop sniffing around, though."

I made it down the stairs first and put my key into the lock of my own apartment, giving her a concerned look. "Do you feel unsafe?"

She snort laughed. "No, it's not like that. He's got a huge dick and he's an eleven in bed. But he's about a four in all other aspects, so I need to stop seeing him. He's a hot liar, but still a liar. When I asked him why he had the word 'never' tatted on his groin, he said he just liked the word, but then I found out it used to say 'eve,' his ex's name, and he had it changed to 'never.' Like, why not just tell me that?"

I pushed the door to my apartment open and Marlowe walked in, grinning at me.

"Oh, wow. Apartment goals."

She took in the hardwood floors I'd dusted and mopped yesterday, and the industrial-style shelving unit with houseplants. As she rocked a still-crying Iris back and forth in her arms, her gaze landed on the corner of my living room where I had my workstation set up.

"You work at that desk? How is it so organized?" Marlowe shook her head, sounding baffled. "Are you a professional organizer? If you are, you're hired."

I smiled. "I'm a lawyer."

She gave me an appraising look and then returned my smile. "Okay, I can see it. You've got that no-nonsense look about you. What kind of law?"

"I own a legal research business."

Marlowe's face lit up. "So you work from home? All the time?"

Well, when babies weren't making it impossible, I did. I nodded in response.

"Girl, me too! I do a podcast." She gave me a pleading look. "Can you show me the bathroom next? I assume it's in the same place mine is. And if you could hold this tiny terror so I can pee, I'd owe you so huge."

My pulse raced as she started passing me the baby. I'd never held a baby before. What if I did it wrong? What if she screamed even louder?

"Oh, I…"

Marlowe didn't seem to notice my hesitation as she nestled Iris into my arms.

"Can you walk back there with me and keep talking so I know you're not taking off with Iris? Josie will fucking kill me if I let her kid get kidnapped on my watch."

Wow. This woman just put her every thought directly into the world. I could see why Never liked her, though. She had beautiful blue eyes, a tiny round silver nose ring, and a natural confidence I wished I had.

"So what's your podcast about?" I asked, following her to the bathroom but stopping before I reached the door.

"It's about women and sex," she answered from inside the bathroom, leaving the door open. "It's called Cliterally Speaking."

Of course it was. Why had I even wondered if

Marlowe would say she liked to talk about history or wellness?

I looked down at the baby in my arms, who was still crying but had her eyes closed. Iris was exhausted. How did her mother ever get anything done while having an infant to care for? What an absolute time suck.

She did have a sweet little nose, though, and perfect little lips. And the cooing sounds she made in between cries made my heart melt.

"What's wrong, Iris?" I asked softly. "Can you tell me?"

She opened her eyes and looked at me, and something inside me shifted. Her soft, beautiful blue gaze locked onto me, and I couldn't look away. Were we having a moment?

"Here, let's try this," I said, gently moving her into an upright position against my chest, her little face peeking over my shoulder.

I'd seen people hold babies like this on TV. Maybe she just wanted a look at the world around her, instead of staring at faces nonstop.

Patting her back, I put my cheek against the side of her head. She was so soft. So tiny. And I couldn't get enough of her fresh, sweet smell.

After several pats on her back, Iris let out a massive sound. It took me a second to register that it was a burp. She immediately relaxed and stopped crying.

"What was that?" Marlowe asked from inside the bathroom, flushing the toilet.

"I think she burped," I said. "It smells like sour milk."

"Oh my god, you're a genius. And I think you should decorate my bathroom when I get unpacked, because yours is gorgeous."

By the sound of the running water, I knew she was washing her hands. I reached over to stroke Iris's tiny hand and she wrapped her fist around my finger and cooed. A tug started inside my chest at knowing my time holding little Iris was almost over. Swallowing hard, I pressed a kiss to the dark, downy hair on top of her head, closing my eyes.

God, this felt amazing. Now that she'd burped, she was drifting off, and all I wanted was to sit down with her and watch her sleep. Sneak in little caresses of her tiny fingers and round cheeks. Kiss her little head over and over. I'd fixed her. I'd comforted this tiny, helpless human. Was there anything more fulfilling?

"Thank you," Marlowe said, emerging from the bathroom and reaching for the baby.

I didn't want to give up Iris just yet, so I led the way back to the living room.

"Do you want some coffee?" I asked.

"I'd love some. I don't know which box my coffee maker is in, so I've been Door Dashing it, but I didn't have time this morning because I had to do an early yoga class."

Her phone dinged and Marlowe read the message on the screen.

"Or not," she said. "Josie's going to be here in ten minutes, and I have to pack up Iris's diaper bag."

She reached for the baby again, and I reluctantly passed her over, missing the feel of her the moment she was gone.

"Do you want to take my number?" Marlowe asked. "I'm new to Denver, and I'd love a local friend to hit up coffee shops and restaurants with."

"Um, sure."

I got my phone and entered her number as she recited it.

"How about lunch Friday?" she asked.

I never went out for lunch on workdays. My thirty-minute break was always spent eating a quick meal, stretching, and doing a five-minute meditation. But truth be told, I never went out for lunch because I never had an invite.

"Okay," I said. "Friday."

"Perf. I'll be doing some day drinking, but no

judgment if you don't want to." She winked at me. "Thanks again for your help, Shelby."

"No problem."

"Say 'bye,' Iris." Marlowe gently took the sleeping infant's slack wrist and moved it in a waving motion.

As soon as I closed the door, I pressed my back against it, reeling from the unexpected emotions welling within me.

My annoyance over Iris's crying was nothing compared to how amazing it felt to have her in my arms. For a moment, it was like I had a family again.

Since the deaths of my grandparents five years ago, I'd been alone in the world. And for the most part, I'd been okay with that. I'd told myself my work was my legacy. But when I'd held Iris, something had...clicked. It was like this hole opened up inside me, or maybe it was there all along and I never realized it. I wasn't just a lawyer. I was a woman. A woman who could soothe a crying baby. A woman who could be a *mother*. And that's when it hit me.

I wanted a baby.

More than anything.

CHAPTER TWO

Three months later

Beau

"Jesus, does Sara Lane want to have your babies or what?"

The derision in my teammate Colby's tone wasn't really about the sports reporter who threw me softball questions at the after-game press conference. He'd had a shit game and was blowing off steam. And I couldn't deny there was some accuracy in his question.

Sara had asked my teammates about their mistakes on the ice tonight, but she'd asked me how it felt to be named one of Denver's Most Eligible Bachelors by a local magazine.

"She asked you the same goddamn question at the last press conference!" Colby scoffed and loosened the tie around his neck as we made our way through the arena's player exit. "I thought her next question would be if you want her to spit or swallow."

"We'll never know since Mike Groban got to ask the next question." I grinned at my friend. "And swallow, obviously."

"You'll find out what it feels like to not be the golden boy anymore someday," Colby grumbled. "I just hope I'm there to see it."

He'd had a *really* bad game tonight, and Coach had put his foot so far up Colby's ass it would be sore for days. Unlike me, Colby wasn't a player who could easily reset himself after a loss.

"Mountain Top?" I asked, proposing a trip to our favorite after-game bar.

He gave me a wry grin. "Yeah. I'll buy since I'm being such an asshole."

I clapped him on the shoulder. "You're always an asshole. It's part of your charm."

He got in the passenger side of my Range Rover, as usual. We both knew he'd be in no condition to drive by the end of the night and he'd either Uber home or crash at my place.

It was a fifteen-minute drive from the arena to the bar, which I probably could have done with my eyes closed since I'd grown up near Denver. I was lucky to be drafted by my hometown team nine years ago, and I hoped I never played anywhere else.

"We should get in a camping trip before it gets any colder," Colby said as I drove.

He was from Indiana, and he was still enthralled with the mountains here. In the two years since he'd been traded to Denver, we'd taken around ten back-packing trips. Some were just a couple of nights, but one we'd done in the off-season had been two weeks.

"Yeah, we should take McCall," I said.

Rowan McCall was our newest teammate, and he and his girlfriend had broken up when he got traded from Tampa. He was entirely focused on hockey, and he needed to get out and live a little.

I parked about a block away from Mountain Top, and on the walk to the bar, snowflakes started swirling in the air around us.

"Bro, it's October," Colby said, shaking his head. "Are we skipping fall?"

"I trick-or-treated in snow boots all the time as a kid."

We were close to the bar's entrance when a small

group of women came up to us, all of them dressed nicely.

"Hey, it's the hockey players," one of them said. "Are you guys going to Mountain Top, too?"

They made it so unbelievably easy. I'd seen these women here before, and it was clear that tonight they weren't taking any chances on other women getting our attention inside the bar by waiting for us out here.

"We are," Colby said, his shit mood apparently forgotten. He smiled at one of the women, extended a hand and said, "Hi, I'm Colby Harrison."

Prick. He'd called dibs on the most attractive woman in the bunch, who told him her name was Lexi. We walked in as a group, and a redhead took my arm, her industrial-strength perfume smelling like a freshly scrubbed toilet. Why did women think that shit was sexy?

Everyone knew the Colorado Coyotes players hung out at Mountain Top after games, and every game we played was shown live on the big screens here. After our shit performance tonight, there was no applause for Colby and me when we walked in, apparently the first players to arrive tonight.

"You suck, Harrison!" someone called from the other side of the rustic-themed bar.

I held back a smile as Colby glowered. Our team

captain, Dalton, always told us if we walked into Mountain Top after a game, we'd better be prepared to hear about every fuckup we made that night. If we weren't up for it, there were lots of other places we could go where we wouldn't be recognized.

"Let's get some drinks," Colby muttered, scooting past Lexi much closer than needed.

"Beau!" a female voice called from nearby. "Over here!"

I looked over to find Tiffany, the unofficial leader of the Foxes, waving me down from a nearby table. Making sure to only sigh inwardly, I waved back.

It was cool having a fan club, I reminded myself. The Foxes were a group of about ten female season ticket holders, ranging in age from thirty to maybe seventy, who brought signs to every home game. Some had my face on them, and others had pictures of socks. Shortly after I started playing for the Coyotes, the Foxes had formed and named them-selves based on my name—Beau Fox. They chanted "Fox Rocks Our Socks" at games and had started a thing where every time I scored a goal, they each threw a sock onto the ice. It had caught on quickly, and now when I scored, the arena crew had to come out and sweep up hundreds of socks.

"You'll get 'em next time!" Tiffany said as I approached their table.

She immediately passed me a Sharpie and pulled down on the collar of her V-neck T-shirt, baring half of her breast. This was their tradition—having me sign their breasts after games.

"Hey, thanks for cheering us on even when we lose," I said, scrawling my signature across her breast for at least the hundredth time.

"Me next," another woman said, pulling her shirt down.

These women were fearless. They gave zero shits who saw most of their breasts as I signed them, and I had to admire them for that.

"Beau, this is our newest Fox, Carla," Tiffany said, gesturing at a woman with white hair who was trying to get her breast into signing position.

It wasn't working so great. She was older, her shirt didn't have a wide neck opening, and her breasts were saggy.

"To hell with it," she said, reaching for the bottom of her shirt.

Shit. I couldn't let a senior citizen raise her entire shirt in a crowded bar. I gently put my hands on her arms to stop her.

"You know what, Carla?" I said. "New members get something special."

I leaned in and kissed her cheek, and she beamed at me, fanning herself.

"I'm sixty-seven, and you just made me feel about twenty again!" she cried.

Winking at her, I finished my rounds and signed all the other breasts, then posed for a photo with the group.

"I'm thirsty, ladies, but I hope to see you at the next game," I said, smiling at them.

"We'll be there!" Tiffany said.

As I ordered at the bar, I casually scanned the crowd. I wasn't specifically looking for a hookup, but I wouldn't say no if the right opportunity presented herself. We were leaving for a road trip the day after tomorrow, and our schedule would be a grind.

When the bartender passed me my beer, I handed him some cash and nodded my thanks. As I turned to walk back toward Colby, I nearly bumped into a twentysomething woman with dark hair. Her brows were drawn together in a serious look, a little line between them.

"Sorry about that," I said.

She just stared at me, her eyes wide behind her black-rimmed glasses. I gave her a polite nod and turned to go.

"I want your sperm," she blurted.

Yikes. There had to be a full moon tonight. I liked women who made it easy, and she wasn't bad looking at all, but I hadn't even had a sip of my beer yet, and I was hungry.

"Listen, I—"

She cut me off, cringing. "That came out wrong. Look, I know you're busy signing…people and all, but could I have just a little bit of your time? I have a question for you that may sound crazy, but…" She gave me a pleading look. "Please."

"Uh, my buddy's waiting for me over there."

"I did more than a month of research—extensive research—on something, and if we could just sit down and talk about it…" The frown line between her brows returned. "You're the only one who can help me, Beau. Please."

This was a new approach. Clearly she wanted to sleep with me, and I'd had women try the hard sell with me before, but not like this. This woman wore a business suit, the dark purple shirt beneath her jacket covering her up to her collarbone.

Wait just a fucking minute. Maybe she wanted to role-play? She'd be the buttoned-up librarian and I'd be…well, me. I looked her up and down. She had a nice body beneath the suit, I could tell. And she played the good girl part to perfection.

I grinned at her. "Okay."

Her shoulders sank with relief. "Thank you. I have a booth over in the corner we can sit at."

I took a long drink from my beer as I followed her, eager to get this show on the road. My gaze locked onto her ass, hidden by a skirt that fell just below her knees. Damn, she'd gone all out with the suit she was wearing. It was about as spinster as a nun's habit.

"Please, have a seat," she said, gesturing to one side of the booth in the corner of the bar.

I slid into my seat, and she did the same on the other side of the booth, folding her hands in front of her on the table.

"My name is Shelby Grant," she said. "I'm twenty-eight and I'm an attorney."

An attorney? Librarian would have been hotter, but I could get into this, too.

"I see." A corner of my mouth quirked up in a smile. "And what will you be charging me with, Miss Grant?"

"What?"

I bit my lip, showing her I was here to play. "Arousal in the first degree? I plead guilty."

She narrowed her eyes in confusion. "Okay, I'm not sure what you're talking about, and I'm not a prosecutor."

"What do you want from me, then?"

She cleared her throat. "I'll start at the end, and then make my case. I just ask that you please,

please give me ten minutes to explain. Can you do that?"

This wasn't feeling very sexy. I shrugged and nodded, just to move things along.

"Okay, so like I said, I want your sperm. Specifically, I want you to be my sperm donor."

My brows shot up in surprise, but I didn't respond. So she did want sex, but she wanted me to get her pregnant? That wasn't just a no. It was a *hell no.*

"I know your instinct is to say no and leave," she continued, passing me a black binder that was sitting on her side of the booth by her coat. "But please take a look at this. I've laid out all the relevant information. My financials, my parenting philosophy, the contract I had drawn up. And of course, you should have your own attorney look it over—at my expense, of course."

I gaped at her, still confused and wondering what the hell was happening.

"Why you?" she asked, straightening her glasses on her nose. "That's what you're thinking, right? Why didn't I just go to a sperm bank and search the available donors and use one of them?"

Actually, I was thinking I wanted to get the hell out of here and get a stronger drink. But Shelby was looking at me so earnestly that I couldn't admit it.

"I…guess, yeah," I said instead.

Her expression brightened. "I did look into existing donors, but I also cross-referenced them with every Most Eligible Bachelor list I could find for the past year. Obviously, I can't ask a married man to donate his sperm. I want someone who is athletic, to counterbalance my complete lack of athleticism. I confined my parameters to men who still have two living parents for genetic reasons. And, Beau…" Her eyes implored me as she spoke. "In every article I read about you, your teammates and coaches said you're always in a good mood. A great friend. Reliable. You're smiling in literally every picture of you online, and there are two thousand one hundred ninety of them, as of last week. Those are qualities I want in my child."

I don't know whether I'm flattered or freaked out by the amount of research she did on me. One thing I do know, though, is that I'm not giving her—or anyone else—my sperm.

"You're about to bolt," she said, apparently reading my expression. "And I get it. I honestly do. All I ask is that you take the binder. I wrote you a letter and included my contact information. There's also the address of a restaurant in there that I'm hoping you'll meet me at for lunch next week so you can ask me any questions you have."

I picked up the binder and gave her a polite nod. "I'll take a look."

When I stand up, she slides out of the booth to stand next to me.

"All I'm asking for is a chance," she says. "Just a chance to tell you more about who I am and why this would mean everything to me."

I gestured at Colby, who was surrounded by women on the other side of the bar. "I have to go join my friends now. But I'll take a look."

"Thank you," she said, giving me a hopeful smile.

I walked across the bar, beer in one hand and binder in the other. When Colby spotted me, he gave me a confused look.

"You doing some homework?" he asked.

I glared at him, no longer in the mood to be in the spotlight that was Mountain Top after a game. Later on, I'd tell Colby I'd not only signed a bunch of boobs tonight, I'd also been asked to father a child.

But for now, I just wanted to finish this beer, followed by a few more.

Shelby

"BUT HE DIDN'T SAY *no*, right?"

Marlowe gave me an encouraging look as she passed me a glass of wine and sat down on the other end of my couch.

"He didn't have to say it. It was all over his face." I took a sip of the wine and made a face. "This tastes terrible."

"Red wine is an acquired taste."

I put my glass on a coaster on the coffee table. "I don't think I want to acquire it."

"We have to find a way to loosen you up, Shelby. Alcohol will help."

"I don't want to loosen up. I just want to have a

baby." I curled up on my end of the couch, still feeling dejected from my conversation with Beau three nights ago.

I knew it sounded crazy. How could a stranger approach someone and ask for their sperm and have it sound anything *but* crazy?

All of it made perfect sense to me, though. In the past three months, I'd not only researched eligible bachelors in the Denver area, I'd also read books on genetics, parenting, and how to make organic baby food. I was well prepared for what to expect, and now I just needed to figure out how to get myself expectant.

"We should go out," Marlowe suggested. "If you let me dress you and do your makeup, you could pick up a guy and possibly be pregnant by midnight."

"It's not the right time in my cycle."

Marlowe hummed. "You could still get in some practice and have a guy to call when it is the right time."

I sat up and gave her an exasperated look. We'd become good friends, and one of the reasons we got along so well was that we always told each other the full truth.

"I'm not looking for a degenerate boyfriend with a name like Rock," I told her. "I want my child to be fathered by a man with good genes."

Marlowe sniffed and looked away, annoyed by my comment about Rock. "Well, you're not going to meet anyone by pouting on the couch."

"Hey, I had a lot of hours invested in researching Beau Fox. It's okay that I'm disappointed it didn't work out."

"What kind of a name is Beau Fox, anyway? It sounds like a porn star name."

"It's the name his parents gave him."

Henry and Claire Fox were the parents of five children; Beau was their third. Claire was a professor of women's studies at the University of Colorado, and the picture of her family I'd seen in an online university magazine was like the template photo for a Christmas card. A beautiful family of eight, including their son-in-law Adrian, stood in front of a stream, snow on the ground and mountains in the background. They wore flannels and vests and boots that were expensive but broken in, clearly not purchased just as props for the photo. All of them had hair in varying shades of brown, Beau's hair among the darkest, and my favorite feature was the matching laugh lines around their eyes and their bright smiles.

The Fox family probably wasn't perfect—no one was. But they loved each other, that much was clear. Beau was part of a big family, every member accomplished in their own right. The joy I saw in their faces was what I wanted for my own son or daughter one day.

"Can we at least go get dinner?" Marlowe asked. "I haven't eaten since breakfast."

I sighed heavily. "Just leave me and my empty womb here to wallow."

"Is this all it takes to bring you down?" Marlowe stood up, rolling her eyes at me. "This is a long road, Shelby. There are going to be disappointments. You approached *one* guy. One." She held out a single finger for emphasis. "And so what? It didn't work out. I happen to know from seeing your color-coded charts that you have lots of other options."

She was right. I knew she was right. I had too much hope wrapped up in Beau Fox, and I needed to let it go and move on.

"I'm waiting for the lunch I invited him to on Wednesday," I said. "If he doesn't show, I'm moving to the next guy."

"Good. Because if this is your dream, don't let anyone discourage you. Keep pushing. You'll get there. Although, again, I don't know what you're thinking." She scowled. "One afternoon of babysitting was enough to make me seriously consider getting my tubes tied."

"I want a baby more than anything."

It had become more than just a want; I yearned for a child of my own. I'd recently walked into a baby boutique and teared up when I picked up tiny white and yellow dressing gowns and caps. The smells of baby powder and lotion made me sigh dreamily and imagine rocking my own freshly bathed infant in the nursery I'd start designing the moment I found out I was pregnant.

Not only didn't I need a relationship with a man to do this, I didn't want one. At all. I wanted this baby to be mine and only mine.

"Can't you want a baby *and* eat dinner?" Marlowe coaxed. "We can talk about baby names if you want."

"Okay." I took a deep breath, getting myself into a better frame of mind. "But we talk about baby stuff all the time. I'd like to hear about how your show went today."

She grinned. "Girl, it was amazing! I interviewed a couple of women in their seventies about their sex lives."

I furrowed my brow. "On second thought, I might not want to hear about that."

"Don't be ageist," Marlowe scolded. "Grandmas like dick just as much as women our age do."

Shaking my head, I went to grab my bag and keys. This was apparently the price I'd have to pay for yapping about fertilization windows and teething nonstop for the past month or so.

Picking up the wineglass I'd discarded, Marlowe downed the entire glass and carried it into my kitchen.

"Did you know pubes turn gray just like regular hair?" she asked over her shoulder.

Dear god. It was going to be a long evening.

———

I GLANCED at my watch and my heart sank. It was 12:35 p.m.—Beau was officially five minutes late to the lunch I'd invited him to in my letter.

Well, he'd be five minutes late if he walked in right this minute. Otherwise, he'd be a no-show.

Though I'd hardly slept last night, I wasn't tired. Adrenaline and too much coffee had me on edge, and my emotions weren't helping any.

I wanted this *so badly*. In every article I'd read about Beau, I'd seen that he was my opposite. A counterbalance to my neurotic, risk-averse person-ality. I didn't want my child to inherit my numerous fears and insecurities, and Beau's genes could only help with that.

He wasn't just easygoing, he was also generous. He visited patients at a local children's hospital and was known for doing random acts of kindness. Last year, he'd heard about a single mom who was struggling and bought her a new car, and he'd tried to keep it quiet but one of her family members had leaked the news.

I didn't care about his playboy reputation, because that part of his life would never touch mine or my child's. As long as he passed the health screening at my doctor's office, I just needed his sperm sample and then he'd be out of my life forever.

"Hey, just checking in," my server said, giving me a gentle smile.

I'd gotten here at 12:05—early as usual. My server was a woman named Lydia who was clearly hip to the fact that I was being stood up.

"I'll keep waiting," I said, trying to sound confident.

"I'll get you some more water," she said.

I'd already gone through two glasses, because I was a stress water drinker. Though at this moment, I wished I was a stress smoker or coke snorter because damn, I needed something to take the edge off.

"Brought you some bread, too," Lydia said when she returned with my water.

Bread! Perfect. Now I had something else to

focus on besides the empty doorway of the restaurant. I pulled a warm, fluffy roll from the basket and fished a rectangular pat of butter from the bottom.

It was just how I liked it—the bread had softened the butter and made it the perfect spreading consistency. It really was the little things that made a person's day. I took my time buttering both sides of the bread, then stretched time further by checking my phone in between bites.

No texts from Beau saying he was running late. But it had been a full twenty minutes since I'd checked news headlines and my email, so I did that.

I tried to get engrossed in an article about the economy, because we should all be knowledgeable about the world around us, right? I told myself that, but in reality, I was crumbling inside.

He wasn't going to show. Deep down, I'd known it was a long shot. He'd been polite the night we met, but also dismissive.

This wasn't the end of the road. Not even close. Now that I knew what I wanted—a family—I wouldn't give up until I had it.

My baby wouldn't have Beau's easy smile or generous spirit, but there were other men out there who could help me have a baby. And no matter who fathered my child, I'd love him or her with everything in me.

"Did you want to order?" Lydia asked me, her gaze loaded with pity.

"No, I think I'll just go, but thanks."

I pulled some cash from my wallet to tip her and set it on the table, then stood up.

"Hey," she said softly. "Whoever he is, screw him. You can do better."

She thought I was being stood up by a romantic partner. Ha—if only. That was so trivial compared to the lead ball I felt like I had in my chest right now.

"Thanks," I said, surprised by the emotion welling in my throat.

"Want some raspberry cheesecake to go?" she asked me. "It's on the house."

There was something about her tone, and about picking up my bag and coat and preparing to leave the restaurant, that got to me. The tears in my eyes didn't even have a chance to well—they just spilled onto my cheeks without warning.

"Thanks, but I'm okay," I said, wiping the corners of my eyes furiously.

"It's going to be okay," Lydia said, wrapping her arms around me in a hug.

"I just really wanted it to work out," I said, disappointment hitting me like a punch to the gut. "I thought...I mean, I hoped..."

Lydia spoke softly. "Fuck men."

"Yeah," I agreed, choking the word out.

People were staring at us, but I didn't care. All my careful planning and preparing over the past three months had built a hope in me that had just been crushed. I wasn't giving up, but I was giving myself a little bit of time to wallow. In the dining room of Tony's Trattoria.

"Hey." Lydia pulled back, her hands on my shoulders and her eyes on mine. "Go home and take a nice bubble bath and put on some fun music. DoorDash a gallon of your favorite ice cream and just read a book or something, okay?"

I nodded and smiled at her. "I will. Thank you."

"You sure about the cheesecake?" She arched her brows. "It's really good, and you deserve it."

I looked at the doorway of the restaurant, and then back at her.

"You want the cheesecake. I can tell," she said. "It'll take me two minutes to grab it and I'll be right back."

I left the little Italian restaurant shortly after that, clutching the handle of a bag with my cheesecake in it and still crying.

CHAPTER FOUR

Beau

Dear Beau,

It must feel so strange to have a woman you don't know ask you to donate sperm. I'll respect your decision either way, but I want to make sure you know more about me before deciding.

I'm not sure where I was born. My mom has bipolar disorder, and she remembered that she was in a hospital when she had me, but she doesn't know where it was. My father was in and out of our lives for those first years, and he wasn't around when I was born. He was an alcoholic who started using drugs and it eventually killed him. I don't tell you these things to make you feel sorry for me, but to show you who I am. My mom and I moved around a lot when I was a kid, because she could never hold down a job. Our entire lives could be packed into her car and driven to a new place on a whim. This meant I never got to stay in school for long, if I was even enrolled in a school, but wherever we moved, I always found a library and read everything I could get my hands on.

Everything changed when I was fifteen. That's when my dad's parents were finally able to find me. They had been trying for years. When they found out how bad things were for me, they moved me into their home in Madison, WI. They hadn't had contact with my father for many years and their hearts were broken by the path he went down, and they told me all the time that having me live with them was the greatest thing that ever happened to them. They were the best people I've ever known. Thanks to them, I was able to enroll in high school and catch up. I had a real home for the first time in my life, and I no longer had to wonder how or when I'd be able to eat next.

I was in my first year of law school at the University of Chicago when my grandparents were killed in a car accident. My whole world died that day. But they left me everything they had in their will, and they'd both written me letters in which they encouraged me to keep going, no matter what happened.

That was five years ago. I moved to Denver after law school, because I had a friend who was here, but she ended up moving for a new job and then I was alone here. I started my own legal research business. As you can see from the financials I provided, I make a great living and have plenty to fall back on thanks to what my grandparents left me.

Having a baby will mean I have a family again. My child will be my entire world. I want to be the mother I never had. I've read dozens of parenting books and gotten certified in infant CPR. If you help me have a child, you'll be changing my life forever.

In case this seems like a backward attempt to start a relationship with you, I assure you it isn't. All I want is the donation and then we'll never see each other again. I've had contracts drawn up that absolve you of all ties to my child, and I'd be happy to pay your attorney to review them on your behalf. One contract stipulates that neither of us ever disclose this arrangement, if you're concerned about that.

If anything I've said sparks your interest in helping me, I'd love to see you Wednesday for lunch at the restaurant I've attached a card for. I'm also including my phone number. Thank you for reading this and considering my request.

Sincerely,
Shelby Grant

. . .

I SET the letter on my kitchen counter after reading it for the fifth time. Since I didn't even look at it until returning from my road trip, I'd missed the lunch. Shelby most likely assumed it was a no from me and would move on.

It had to be a no. Didn't it? I left Mountain Top that night sure I'd just met my craziest fan yet. If I'd seen a trash can on the walk back to my car, I would have dropped the binder into it and never looked back.

Sheer curiosity made me open it and look at the contents. Shelby had used color-coded tabs to divide it into sections, and she'd included everything from her college transcripts to paint samples and decor ideas for a baby nursery.

Flipping through the pages and skimming them, I'd started to see her less as crazy and more as... determined. She wasn't sitting back and hoping for her dream to come true; she was actively grinding to make it a reality. The athlete in me admired that. There wasn't a doubt in my mind that Shelby would have the baby she wanted so badly. The only question was, would I be the biological father?

It wouldn't hurt to have my attorney look things over, especially if she was paying for it. Part of me—a big part—was flattered to be her top choice. She knew I was a total package.

My parents had drilled using protection during sex into me as a teenager, and I'd used it every time. I helped condom manufacturers stay in business, because in the decade I'd been having sex, I'd used...*a lot* of condoms.

This would be a chance to see what it felt like without one. *Trying* to get a woman pregnant—that was hard to imagine as a bachelor who couldn't imagine myself having kids.

What if I never got married and had my own family? If I stayed healthy and played hockey as many years as my body let me, there was a real possibility I'd never settle down.

Shelby's kid could come find me one day as an adult and be the only child I ever fathered.

I rubbed a hand down my face. Shit. This was a lot to think about. I liked to keep things light, and this was anything but.

After twisting off the cap on a bottle of beer, I sat down to catch up on shows I'd missed while on my road trip, but I couldn't shake the things Shelby had said in the letter.

You'll be changing my life forever. Having a baby will mean I have a family again.

I had a big family, and sometimes they were a pain in my ass, but I couldn't imagine my life without them. On a whim, I picked up my phone and texted the number Shelby had included in her letter.

Hey, it's Beau. Sorry I missed lunch, I was on a road trip. Can we reschedule?

She responded immediately.

Yes! Anytime, just let me know and I'll be there.

I couldn't believe I was seriously considering doing this, but I was. I wrote back.

I'll ask my attorney to look at what you sent and then text you to meet for lunch at the same place you wanted to meet up before. That work for you?

Again, she responded immediately.

Yes. Thank you.

———

THREE DAYS LATER, I approached Shelby, who was sitting alone at a table in a little downtown Italian place called Tony's Trattoria. She beamed at me, her eyes hopeful.

"Hi," I said, sitting down across from her. "You picked a good place. This is one of my mom's favorites."

"Well, I can confirm they have great cheesecake," she said.

She sounded nervous and looked it, too, her back perfectly straight and her hands in her lap.

"They have good red wine, too," I suggested, because she looked like she could use a glass to loosen up.

"None for me, but order some for yourself if you want." She looked at the menu. "They sell it by the bottle, so order a whole bottle if you want."

I could tell Shelby would've bought me an entire case of wine if it would help me agree to her proposal. She wanted this so damn badly. I'd seen this same look on the faces of guys who got called up from the minors. They wanted to prove themselves and live their dreams more than anything.

"No, I'm good," I said, nodding at our server as she approached.

Shelby ordered water and a grilled chicken salad; I went for lasagna and unsweetened tea. Once the server had left us alone at the table, Shelby just looked at me expectantly, waiting for me to tell her if I was in or out.

I cleared my throat. "So my attorney looked the paperwork over and said it protects me in every way legally possible."

"I swear I don't want anything from you except… you know."

"My attorney said even though it protects me, he still advises against it."

Shelby deflated. "I understand."

This was my last chance to bow out gracefully. I could make small talk with her, pick up the lunch check, and wish her well with her dream. That wasn't what my gut told me to do, though.

"I'm in," I said.

She looked up from the table, a little line of confusion forming between her brows. "What do you mean?"

"I mean, yes," I said, grinning. "Let's do this. I'll help you have a baby."

Her eyes flooded with tears. "Oh my god, are you serious?"

"I am. I've given it a lot of thought and read your letter about fifty times. If you're completely sure you want to do this alone and all you need is for me to get you pregnant, I'll do it."

She covered her face with her hands, crying. I didn't know what to say, so I just sat there, uncomfortable even though they were happy tears.

A woman wearing the red polo and nametag of a Tony's server approached our table, her furious gaze locked on me.

"Is this him?" she demanded. "Is this the guy who stood you up?"

Shelby took her hands away from her face, looking surprised. "Lydia."

"If this jerk is making you cry two weeks in a

row, you need to get up and leave right now," the server said. "He's not worth it."

What was this? How had I made Shelby cry last week?

Oh. When I didn't show up for lunch. Shit. She'd been here hoping I'd show up and left thinking I just hadn't bothered to show up or say anything.

"No," Shelby assured the server. "These are happy tears, I promise. He's giving me something incredible. It's not what you think."

Lydia gave me a skeptical look, then met Shelby's gaze again. "Okay. But I'm here if you need anything, okay?"

Shelby smiled gratefully. "Thanks, I appreciate it."

After we were alone again, an awkward silence fell between us.

"Sorry about that," Shelby finally said.

"It's okay." I glanced at my watch. "I have to pick my niece up from preschool, so I need to get out of here by one at the latest. Do you want to make plans while we're here? We can get a hotel room if you want."

Her eyes widened in abject shock. "What? No, no, no." She quickly composed herself. "Sorry, that's my fault. I should have explained better. You'll make your donation at my doctor's office, and then she'll take it from there."

Huh. I'd been thinking she wanted to do this the old-fashioned way, but apparently not. It was probably for the best, given how uptight she was.

"Sure," I said, shrugging. "However you want to do it."

"I'll send you the number for the doctor's office and you can schedule an appointment whenever it works for you."

I nodded, trying to think of a tactful way to pose my question to her.

"Hey," I said, meeting her gaze with a smile. "I'm not an asshole. If you have a partner that you want to include in all this, you don't need to worry that I'm some kind of bigot. I support LGBTQ rights and marriage equality."

She shook her head. "It's not that, Beau. I'm not gay, but I'd tell you if I were. I'm attracted to men and only men, but I want to keep this transactional. I think sex could…muddy things."

She was right. Hell, it could take multiple tries to get her knocked up, and what if she got hooked on the sex? Women usually caught feelings from sleeping together, no matter what arrangements were agreed upon up front.

This was a smart approach. She couldn't get her heart broken this way.

"Okay then," I said, smiling. "I'll make an appointment."

"Thank you so much, Beau. I can't believe this is happening. I'm so happy."

It was the first time I'd made a woman glow by *not* having sex with her. This was unlike anything I'd ever imagined myself doing. It couldn't have been any easier, though. All I had to do was get off to make Shelby's dream come true.

I could most definitely do that.

CHAPTER FIVE

Shelby

IF THIS WAS what first date nerves felt like, I wanted no part of it. Not that men were clamoring to take me out, but if they were, my response would have been, "Meh."

Though I wasn't waiting for Beau to show up for a date, my stomach was churning like I was. Checking the doorway, then my watch, then the doorway again.

What if he changed his mind? Panic filled my chest. It had been nearly three weeks since Beau agreed to do this, and other than his text to me about the appointment today and my text last night reminding him about it, we hadn't had any contact.

Three weeks was a lot of time for reflection. I'd kept busy working, reading more parenting books, and starting prenatal care. For the first week of daily exercise, no caffeine, and prenatal vitamins, I was on cloud nine. I was preparing to get pregnant with a child of my very own, which made my dream feel one step closer to reality.

During week two, though, I started to seriously miss my coffee. I knew it would be okay for me to have a little, but I wasn't taking any chances. Baby Grant deserved to grow in the most hospitable womb possible.

Beau's appointment was in two minutes. I said a silent prayer and looked at the doorway again, but he wasn't walking through it.

Maybe he had called the doctor's office to let them know he was running late. I hadn't actually told him I'd be here today, so he wouldn't have had a reason to tell me if he wouldn't be on time.

I picked up my bag from the chair next to mine and walked to the front desk. While waiting in line, someone tapped me on the shoulder. My heart raced hopefully.

"Hey," Beau said, smiling when I turned around. "I didn't know you were coming." His grin turned into a smirk. "Or maybe we both are?"

He had the jokes. Returning his smile, I met his

gaze, my whole body relaxing with relief to see him here. "I figured I'd just be here for moral support. Didn't want to miss it."

He furrowed his brow, looking concerned, and lowered his voice. "Am I going to have to do this in front of a doctor? I'm not sure I'll be able to, you know…"

Oh, he'd be ejaculating today. I didn't care what I had to do to make it happen. *It was happening.* I'd put up a privacy curtain or download porn onto my phone for him if needed.

I cleared my throat. "We'll make sure…conditions are favorable."

He nodded, looking relieved.

"Hey," I said softly. "Have you abstained for at least forty-eight hours?"

He looked over each of his shoulders to make sure no one was within earshot. "Yep. I did everything they told me to do when I made the appointment. Hope they have an extra-large cup for my load."

I'd wondered if a playboy like him would mind not coming for forty-eight to seventy-two hours before donation day. He was given a lot of medical testing by the Coyotes' team doctor, and the records he'd provided had helped clear some of the preliminary testing required by my doctor's office. Beau had passed all the required health screenings, and I was beyond eager to get things moving. It already felt like I'd been waiting forever.

We reached the front of the line and Beau greeted the receptionist before I had a chance to.

"Good morning, Dani," he said, apparently reading her nametag. "Beau Fox. I have an appointment at one fifteen."

Ugh. What a time to be flirting. But I had a feeling flirting was like breathing for him—he did it without even thinking about it.

Dani looked back and forth between us, probably trying to figure out who I was to him. She was young and attractive. Beau could picture her while he jerked his gherkin if he wanted to; I didn't care. Hell, he could take her out tonight for all I cared—as long as he made his donation.

"Do you want your partner in the room with you?" Dani asked Beau.

"No," I answered for him. "I'll wait out here."

"Okay, you can have a seat, then," she said.

Reluctantly, I walked away from the window, found a chair, and sat down. I didn't want to sit right next to anyone, and I had to go all the way to the other side of the waiting room where I couldn't hear a single thing that was happening at the window. I didn't like it. I wanted to be as involved as I could in the process, though I drew the line at watching Beau masturbate.

To calm my racing pulse, I looked at photos of designer nurseries. Marlowe was going to help me thrift and shop for everything I'd need for a nursery once I got past my first trimester.

My doctor had prepared me for reality—I might not get pregnant on the first try. Or the second. This could be a long road of Beau jerking off into cups and me praying the procedure worked. And once I did get pregnant, there was always a possibility of miscarriage.

Having my hopes crushed would be hard, but I was prepared. I knew what disappointment felt like; I'd experienced a lot of it. I'd cry as many tears as it took to end up with a baby in my arms one day.

"Shelby."

I looked up from the photos of a Harry Potter-themed nursery to see Beau standing in front of me, his expression what I expected it to be after finally getting to relieve his pent-up frustration.

"Can you…?" He nodded in the direction of the hallway that led to the bathrooms.

"Yeah, of course."

I put my phone in my bag and followed him, the nervous churning back in my stomach. For the hundredth time, I worried he'd changed his mind.

Would today be another disappointment to add to my list?

Once we were alone in the hallway, he crossed his arms and looked away, his brow furrowed.

"I can't do it," he said, his tone so low I could barely make out his words.

I closed my eyes. This was what absolute disappointment felt like. I'd thought we were past the point of decision-making.

"You changed your mind," I said, sighing.

"No, it's not that. It's that *I can't*," he hissed out, trying to whisper. "They put me in this little room with all these magazines, but I'm not putting my hands on a magazine that countless other guys have jerked off to. It's just…sterile and even though it's soundproof, I feel like people are watching me and listening."

"Oh." I looked up at him hopefully. "So it's not that you don't want to, but that you *can't*."

He shook his head, his eyes dark with either anger or frustration. "I'm sorry, Shelby, but"

"No. We're not giving up."

He glared at me. "Why don't you go in there and masturbate? It's not easy. I'm used to having an attractive woman begging for it, not some sticky magazine with women in slutty nurse's costumes."

I'd gotten this far, and I wasn't about to give up.

"Let me try," I said, my heart hammering.

His brows shot up in surprise. "You?"

Clutching the handle of my bag so hard my fingers tingled, I nodded. "Give me two minutes to use the bathroom and then I'll go in there with you."

The corners of his lips quirked up. "Is there a section in your binder about the male erection?"

I scowled, unamused by his derision. "Will you just give me two minutes?"

He put his hands up in surrender. "Yeah, fine."

Once inside a bathroom stall, I called Marlowe, praying she'd answer.

"Hey, did you get the spunk?" she asked.

"Not yet," I whispered. "This is an emergency. I need to know how to turn a man on, and quickly."

"Why? Does this guy expect you to jerk him off? Because I don't think that's how"

"Marlowe, I don't have time. Please. Tell me what you know because I have no idea. I've never done this. How do I make him come?"

There was a pause on the other end of the phone, and then, "Okay. So, you can easily do this by just talking to him if you do it right. Make it all about him and his cock. If it's more than…I don't know, like six inches when he's hard, call it his *big cock*. Tell him you've been fantasizing about having his big cock in your wet pussy."

"Oh, Jesus." I cringed just thinking about saying it.

"And be breathy. Moan if it feels right. Tell him he makes your nipples hard and you want to suck his big cock, ride his big cock, and take his big cock in all your holes."

I groaned with disgust. No wonder I was a virgin. This sounded horrible.

"Are you sure this will work?" I whispered, hearing someone else walk into the bathroom.

"Yes, but you have to sell it. Make him believe you want his cock so bad you can't survive without it. Think about something you really do want and pretend you're talking about that."

A baby. I wanted a baby that badly.

"Okay, I have to go," I said. "Thanks."

"Oh, and tell him you want him to come on your face. They love that."

"Ugh. Goodbye."

"Bye, babe. Good luck."

I ran from the bathroom back out to the hallway, wondering if Beau would still be there. He was leaning against the wall and looking at his phone.

"Let's do this," I said, sounding a lot more confident than I felt.

He gave me a skeptical look, but then turned and led the way to a small, white room that *did* feel incredibly sterile. There was a wood rack on the wall filled with magazines with well-worn covers I wouldn't have wanted to touch, either. A round plastic cup with a lid and a paper bag sat on a shelf.

"Listen, Shelby, if you try to do this, you're going to think the problem is you, but it's not. I just can't relax here."

"Try," I said, a note of pleading in my tone. "Just try, please."

He looked reluctant, but nodded.

"I'm shy about this stuff," I said, which was a dramatic understatement. "So I want to talk to you, but I don't want us to look at each other while I do it."

"Okay."

He walked over to the shelf where the container was and opened it, then started to unfasten his jeans. My pulse skyrocketed. I raced over to stand next to him, closing my eyes and speaking as close as I could get to his ear. He was so much taller than me that I was talking to his shoulder, though.

Think about the baby, Shelby. Think about how much you want your baby.

"I...like your big cock," I managed, dying inside. "It's really nice and I want it inside me."

"Okay," Beau said softly. "I can work with that. Tell me more."

I tried to remember exactly what Marlowe had said, but I was so nervous that it all jumbled together. My dream of a family was dependent on my ability to be sexy, and that was laughable.

"I want your big cock in all my holes," I said, already running short on material. "And I want you to come on my face."

Beau sighed softly. "Look, I appreciate you trying, but I can't do this. Not here. Not like this."

My dreams of a child with his beautiful blue eyes were slipping away. I ignored Marlowe's advice and turned to my gut instead.

"Beau, I'm a virgin," I said, my voice hardly above a whisper. "I'm not sexy and experienced because I've never done anything before."

He pulled back slightly and met my gaze. "Nothing?"

I shook my head, my cheeks heating. It was time to put it all on the line—everything I had.

"But if I could lose my virginity to you…" I licked my lips and put a hand on my cheek. "I know it would be good. You'd make it good." I slid my hand down to my neck, across my collarbone, to one of my breasts. "You'd undress me so slowly, and be patient with me as I ran my hands over your chest and arms, down to the waistband of your jeans. I'd fumble getting them undone and when I finally got to feel you, I'd close my eyes and take my time, running my hand up and down your cock. You'd groan with pleasure and kiss me, wanting more but knowing you'd have to take your time with me."

I was light-headed, knowing I was completely out of my element. It would have been easier for me to lecture on any of the constitutional amendments without any prep than to do this, but it was doing… something. Beau had pushed down his jeans and his eyes were narrowed. And his hand was…occupied.

"You'd teach me," I said, my gaze locked onto his. "You'd tell me to get on my knees and take you in my mouth, and I'd just want to please you. You'd teach me how to make you crazy, but you wouldn't let yourself come. First, you'd touch me and tease me as long as it took for me to beg you for more. You would enjoy that."

"Yeah." His tone was low and he was breathing harder.

"You'd be going crazy, but making yourself go so slowly," I continued. "Wanting to come so badly, but not wanting to hurt me. You'd always make sure I came first. Every time. Even if you were out of your mind, you'd make me come first. And you'd know exactly how to do it. With your fingers or your mouth, and just seeing how turned on you were, I'd come exactly when you told me"

"Oh, *fuck*." He tensed all over and then his shoulders dropped and he met my gaze.

I waited, trying to decipher the look he was giving me, but not wanting to look down either. "Did you…?"

"Oh, yeah. You're good at that."

I grinned, my mortification already forgotten. Somehow, I'd done it. Sheer force of will had made me find a way to make Beau come.

I was another step closer to being a mother.

CHAPTER SIX

Beau

I PARKED my Range Rover in the driveway of my parents' home, smirking at my older brother's minivan.

Asher was thirty-two to my twenty-seven, but he'd gotten married six years ago and now had two kids, and all the chaos that came with them. I loved my niece and nephew but I was reminded how much work kids are the moment I walked in the door of the sprawling log home that was now the Fox family home base.

Four-year-old Anderson ran past me, completely naked except for the red superhero cape floating behind him as he ran, secured around his neck. He was carrying a foam dart launcher, his expression as intent as an actual soldier on a hunt.

"Asher, put your underwear back on!" my sister-in-law, Chloe, called from another room. "And no shooting darts at faces!"

He was probably chasing after Isaac, my twenty-five-year-old brother. There were five of us—Asher, Fiona, who was twenty-nine, I fell right in the middle, then there was Isaac, and Genevieve was twenty-three. Gen was away at medical school, but the rest of us had stayed in the area where we grew up.

"And there's Beau." My mom smiled at me as I walked into the enormous kitchen. "Hi, honey."

"Hey, Mom. Smells great in here."

She took a break from whatever she was chopping at the island to give me a hug.

"I made lasagna. Hope you're hungry."

I patted my stomach. "Always."

My older sister walked into the room, looking a little disoriented. "Sorry, Mom, I fell asleep. What can I help with?"

Mom nodded at the stools pulled up to the kitchen island. "Nothing. Just sit down."

"Are you sick?" I asked Fiona.

"I don't think so. Pregnancy is just exhausting. Some nights I get home from work and throw together a quick dinner and I'm in bed within an hour."

She was four months along with her first child, and her job as CFO of a tech company was demanding.

"Why doesn't Adrian cook dinner?" I asked, grabbing a slice of cucumber from the big bowl of salad my mom was putting chopped vegetables in.

"He works, too," Fiona said, a defensive note in her tone.

Chloe, Asher's wife, had fit in with our family immediately. My parents accepted Adrian, but Asher, Isaac, and I weren't his biggest fans. He was a tool, and I had a feeling Fiona would be responsible for most of the parenting work, just like she was for all the cooking and cleaning.

"Is Adrian going to make it over to eat with us?" Mom asked Fiona.

"No, he's pretty tired from the bachelor party. I told him I'd bring some food home for him."

"There's my favorite middle son!" My dad walked into the kitchen and hugged me. "What's going on with you, Beau?"

I shrugged. It had been three weeks since I'd met Shelby at the doctor's office for my sperm donation. I knew better than to tell my parents about it. My father was an attorney and he'd definitely freak and start thinking of all the worst-case scenarios he could come up with. So even though Shelby and her potential pregnancy were on my mind, I couldn't tell anyone about it.

"Just hockey and more hockey," I said.

"What the hell was up with that hit by Kline the other night?" Asher asked as he walked into the family room, which was open to the kitchen.

I furrowed my brow. "I don't remember it."

"He slammed Harrison's head into the boards. No call."

"Oh, yeah." I nodded, remembering watching that hit on highlight film our video coordinator put together for all of us. "Kline's the king of cheap shots."

"Where were the refs?"

Asher was trying to be a dude talking sports with another dude, but he was holding his daughter Amara, and she was trying to insert her pacifier into his mouth.

"No thanks, Mar," he said, turning his face away. "Daddy's a big boy. He doesn't need that."

I exchanged a smile with Fiona. Fatherhood had turned our brother into a softie. This was the same guy who had thrown a massive weekend-long party for me in Vegas when I turned twenty-one and ended up in the hospital with alcohol poisoning. He refused to admit that's what happened though—according to Asher, he had been admitted to the hospital for dehydration. But according to his wife, who had been with him for the entire hospital stay, it was alcohol poisoning.

"Are you sure I can't help with anything, Claire?" Chloe asked my mom, walking into the kitchen.

Mom shook her head. "Honey, you spend all week taking care of Asher and the kids. On Sundays, I want you to just relax and let me make you a nice meal."

Asher frowned. "Hey, I help with the kids. As soon as I get home from work, I take over."

Chloe walked over to him and hugged his side while giving him a kiss on the cheek. "Yes, you do, babe. And I appreciate you."

"It's not a favor to you when he parents," my dad reminded Chloe. "Your kids are every bit as much his responsibility as yours."

Mom was a women's studies professor, and she'd been drilling equality into us since we were in the womb. Even when she took a few years away from teaching to take care of us when we were young, my dad was either at work or helping with us.

"You're right," Chloe said, looking up at Asher. "Which reminds me, will you go tell your son to put his underwear on? I think Isaac has him convinced that he pees on your mom's houseplants and I don't want him trying it."

Mom set her knife down on the cutting board, frowning. "Isaac, get in here!"

"Ohh, Isaac's in trouble," Fiona said, smirking.

My dad went over to the fridge and grabbed three beers, then nodded toward the family room, where he had the football pregame show on. Asher and I followed. It would be the perfect spot to not be in the middle of Isaac getting his ass chewed out, but still be able to hear it going down.

––––––––

"Are you shitting me?"

Asher studied my face after asking the question, trying to figure out if I was bluffing or not.

I glared at him. "Why would I make it up?"

He ran a hand down his face. "I don't know, man, it's just…"

We were sitting in chairs on my parents' back deck about an hour after eating. Chloe had joined Anderson and Amara for a nap in one of the guest rooms upstairs, leaving Asher with some time for a private conversation.

I needed someone to talk to about Shelby, and he was my brother. We'd always been close and I trusted him entirely. I didn't want to defend my decision to him, though.

"I don't regret doing it," I said. "I thought about it a lot."

"Yeah, but she could come after you later, man. Legally. And you have a lot to go after."

"My attorney looked over the contract. He said I'm good."

Asher nodded. "Okay. I'm glad there's a contract. But what if something happens to her down the road? Who does the kid go to?"

"That'll be up to her." I took a long sip of beer before looking back at my brother. "Look, I shouldn't have brought it up. Let's talk about something else."

"No, I'm glad you told me."

I gave him a pointed look. "I don't want anyone finding out about this. Not even Chloe."

"I won't tell a soul," Asher assured me. "You have my word."

With a nod, I looked out at the mountains in the distance. Even though this was my home, traveling to other cities for hockey made me appreciate where I lived. Trees, open skies, and mountains relaxed me. Nature was the ultimate reminder that we were just a speck in the grand scheme of things.

"I shouldn't have interrupted you," Asher said. "I

think you had a point to make that I never let you get to."

He was right, but I was aggravated now. I'd been trying to convince myself for three weeks to just forget about Shelby and move on. It wasn't working.

"She's not the type of woman I usually go for," I said.

"No whiskers and bushy tail?" Asher quipped, one of his usual jabs about puck bunnies.

"Part of what I was going to say was whether I'd want to…" I looked over both shoulders to make sure we were still alone. "You know, conceive the kid with her. I thought we might be looking at multiple times and she's…a very uptight attorney."

Asher scoffed. "Say no more. I get it."

"But then when I went to the clinic and…" I shook my head and looked away, regretting my decision to talk to him. "Never mind, man."

"Hey," Asher said. "Whatever it is, it's okay. I'll turn off the sarcasm and just listen."

I turned back to him. Maybe saying what I was feeling would help me move on. I sure as hell needed to.

"I couldn't do what I needed to do in the room at the doctor's office, you know," I said. "So, Shelby, she…*talked to me.*"

Asher furrowed his brow, confused.

"You know, she *talked to me*," I repeated. "To get me into it."

"Oh." Asher nodded appreciatively. "Got it."

"And I fucking came in record time, man. It was what she was saying and hearing *her* say it. And now I can't stop thinking about it. About her. I fantasize about her all the time."

My brother's lips turned up in a small smile. "The woman you weren't sure you'd be able to sleep with."

I sighed heavily. "Yeah, joke's on me, right? I tried to go home with a woman in Vancouver last week and I couldn't even get hard. She was just so…not Shelby."

"This sounds like a mental cockblock," Asher said.

"Yeah, no shit. It's obviously not physical. But what do I do?"

"I'm no psychiatrist," Asher said. "Wait, yes I am."

He laughed, but I didn't, because he'd worn that joke out years ago.

"I think your mind is preoccupied with your last encounter with her," he said. "You need to see her again. Talk about anything but sex. Try to drop in on her when she's not expecting you. She might be annoyed, which would be good, because then *that* will be what your mind recalls as your most recent encounter."

I just looked at him for a few seconds. "Really? This is what twelve years of college and medical school taught you?"

"You never said you wanted my professional advice. I thought this was just brothers shooting the shit."

"Do you have any professional advice?"

He shrugged. "Honestly, I recommend therapy. You could benefit from talking to someone about what kind of woman you're attracted to and why."

"I'm not going to therapy."

"I still have to bill you for a full hour since you asked," he quipped.

"You're an asshole."

"You've got unresolved feelings, Beau. So resolve them. Maybe you should sleep with her. If it's not great, you'll have the closure you need."

"And if it is great?"

He chuckled. "It won't be. You're a twenty-seven-year-old professional athlete. You're nowhere near ready to settle down."

"No, I'm not."

The sound of a door opening made us both turn. Isaac stood in the open doorway, looking between us. "You guys are missing a great game in here."

I stood up. "We'll come back in. My nuts are frozen anyway."

"You're a pussy," Isaac said. "I love this weather."

As a trail and fly-fishing guide, Isaac spent more time outside than inside. The only way he'd ever settle down was if he found a woman who wanted to travel as much as he did and who wouldn't stick her nose up at sleeping in a tent.

"That's why you'll end up married to a Squatch," I said, patting him on the shoulder.

"Mother Nature is my bride."

I scoffed. "Good luck getting head, man."

Once inside, my brothers each opened another beer, but I switched to water. I needed to be sharp for practice in the morning. Isaac was right—it *was* a good game, but my mind was elsewhere.

I was thinking about Shelby Grant and wondering how she relaxed on days off. I had some specific ideas for relaxing her.

Maybe Asher was right. I was fantasizing about her words. If I could experience the real thing, that would provide the closure I needed to move on.

I needed to reach out to Shelby. Get to know her. And hopefully, convince her to let me be her first.

CHAPTER SEVEN

Shelby

"HEY GUYS, welcome to Cliterally Speaking. I'm Marlowe Hill and today we're talking about something you don't hear much about. Dat. Ass. Every woman has her own opinion on butt play and anal sex, and my guest today happens to be a fan. Allie Montgomery is single and dating in New York. She's a beauty influencer and she has an amazing blog called *Allie in the City*. Allie, welcome to the pod."

I'd blocked out two hours of work for book-keeping this afternoon, and I liked listening to Marlowe's podcast when I didn't have to be totally focused on my research. This one sounded…interesting.

"I like it with the right partner," Allie commented. "No woman likes having her delicate backdoor jackhammered, right?"

"God, that's the worst," Marlowe agreed. "Preparation and lube are essential."

I cringed, wondering what I'd gotten myself into. Though I'd never done it, I'd read enough books and seen enough movies to be intrigued by sex. Anal, though, did not look like fun. At least not for the recipient.

"So let's talk about butt play," Marlowe says. "I like both giving and receiving. What about you?"

"Oh, same. But my boyfriend knows I want both of us to shower beforehand if butt play is on the agenda. I'm not getting anywhere near a dirty ass."

Marlowe laughed. "You guys have an agenda?"

"Sometimes we do! If my boyfriend sends me sexy texts during the day about wanting to do something in bed that night, we usually do."

"You're a better girlfriend than I am," Marlowe cracked. "That's probably why I'm single."

"It's all about being with the right partner," Allie said. "Anal with an inexperienced partner is the worst. You don't even want to sit down the next day."

"Ugh." I shook my head as I input my expenses for last month on my laptop.

Why did women participate in something so gross and painful? I planned to keep supporting my friend by listening to her podcasts, but my mind wandered as the discussion continued.

It was too soon to take a pregnancy test, but I'd gotten the procedure done at my doctor's office last week and I could be pregnant. She'd cautioned me about getting my hopes up, telling me it often took multiple tries, but I couldn't help daydreaming and placed a hand on my stomach.

It was early November, which meant there was a possibility I'd become a mother next summer. Since I wasn't sure how many times I'd be able to talk Beau into donating sperm if I needed more, I was hoping to get pregnant quickly.

Though I was recording my insurance expenses, I really wanted to grab my phone and search for baby clothes. I couldn't, though, because I'd made a deal with myself—no buying any more baby clothes until I was pregnant.

I finished recording my expenses and went into the kitchen to make lunch—a turkey and veggie panini. I was in the middle of cleaning up when I heard a knock on my door.

It had to be Marlowe. She was the only one who ever came over. I wondered if she ever listened to her own podcasts. This was a good time to find out since I had the volume on her podcast about *anal sex* cranked up in the other room. I still couldn't wrap my head around it.

When I opened the door, though, it wasn't Marlowe standing there, but Beau.

"Hey." He gave me the confident grin I'd seen in so many of his photos online when researching him.

How I hoped for a little boy with that smile. Or a girl. The gender didn't matter, as long as my child got his bright-blue eyes and easy smile.

"Hi."

What was he doing here? I didn't want to be rude by asking, but I was also dying to know. If he wanted his sperm back, he was too late.

"Your address was on the contract," he said. "I just wanted to stop by and see how you're doing."

Yup. He wanted the sperm back but didn't know how to say it. I needed to handle this carefully, because I wanted to be able to approach him for another sample if I needed to. Maybe several more.

"Oh." I stepped back and opened the door wider. "Do you want to come in?"

"Sure."

He stepped inside and I closed the door behind him, locking the dead bolt as I did every time. Somehow, though, I knew I was safe around Beau. There were so many times since we'd met that he could have laughed at me or rejected me, but he hadn't. Men who were careful not to hurt feelings usually respected people in other ways, too.

"You have to be careful, though," Marlowe's voice blasted out of my computer, where I had the podcast playing. "I once got caught up in the moment and came super close to sucking a shitty dick. Thank Jesus the smell of the shit stopped me. Once the dick goes in your ass, it can't go anywhere else."

"Holla," Allie said. "Shitty dicks go straight to the shower."

"Oh my god." My face burned as I ran over to the computer and closed out the app. "I don't...I mean, I was only listening to it because it's my friend Marlowe's podcast."

He grinned, looking like he was on the verge of laughing. "Hey, it's all good."

I had to be doing a full-body blush right now. Beau and I had shared a few intimate moments at the doctor's office, but I didn't want him to think I was into ass play. Or whatever the kids called it these days.

"Wow, I like your place," he said, walking into the living room. "It's so clean and organized."

"Thanks."

He walked over to my workspace, a nook in the living room with a sizable desk, a bookshelf, and several big potted plants lined up in front of a large window.

"This is where you work?"

"Yeah. I don't need a big office. I like being out here where it's bright."

"You said you do legal research, right?"

"Right."

"So what are you working on?"

I glanced at my desk, trying to remember if I'd left anything confidential sitting out. Really, any paper involving work for a client was confidential, as was the work I did. But I could tell Beau about it in broad terms.

"I'm looking into legal precedents in environmental civil suits."

"Huh. Is it interesting?"

I shrugged. "It is to me. But I know a lot of people find legal research dry."

A lot of people found not just my work, but *me* to be dry, to put it mildly. A few years ago, I'd gone on a couple of dates with a man who told me, while breaking things off, that the tax seminars he was forced to attend were more fun than I was. So I couldn't figure out why Beau, who had his own fan club, had stopped by my apartment. Unless...

"You can't have your sperm back," I blurted. "It's already...in use."

He arched his brows, looking amused. "You think I came here to try to get the sperm back?"

I just looked at him for a few seconds before asking, "Didn't you?"

"No, Shelby. I just wanted to see how you're doing."

I shifted on my feet, less suspicious than I'd been when he arrived. "I'm feeling pretty impatient, to be honest. I could be pregnant but it's too soon to know."

"Have you felt sick at all? Had tenderness in your breasts?"

I lowered my brows and crossed my arms over my chest at the mention of my breasts. Beau just continued to look both amused and unaffected.

"My sister Fiona is pregnant," he said. "So we all get to hear about that stuff."

"Oh." I felt a swirl of joy on his sister's behalf. "How far along is she?"

He considered. "About halfway, I think. Four months?"

"How exciting. Does she have other children?"

He shook his head. "This is her first."

"Wow." I put my hand on my stomach, hoping I was close to having a baby of my own.

"You want to get some lunch?" Beau asked.

I looked over at my desk, where my afternoon of

work was waiting. I stuck to my schedule faithfully, so even though I wanted to stay on good terms with Beau, work took precedence.

"I already ate," I said. "And I have a status update due at the end of the day for the job I'm working on."

He nodded and looked down at his phone. There were probably at least a hundred other women's phone numbers in there he could ask out to lunch. I assumed he was scrolling his options, but he surprised me.

"I'm just checking my schedule. Looks like I've got a work thing tomorrow and then I'm leaving for a road trip. What about Monday night? Are you free for dinner?"

What did he really want? I was terrible at this dance people did when they wanted something, because I was a direct communicator.

"Is there something you want to tell me?" I asked, anxiety rushing through my veins. "Do you not want to give me any more samples? Or is there something you want changed in the contract? Because you don't have to take me out for dinner. You can just tell me. Otherwise, I'll worry until"

He cut me off. "Shelby. I just want to spend some time with you, that's all. I'm invested in your dream, too. We should at least be friends, don't you think?"

No, I didn't think we should. The last thing I

wanted was for Beau to be invested, because that could lead to him wanting to be part of my child's life later.

"Sure," I lied. "Dinner Monday night sounds good."

"Is there any place you really like?"

I shook my head. "We can go anywhere, but I'm not eating raw fish or fried foods or drinking alcohol in case I'm pregnant. I can't be around cat litter boxes, either, because of toxoplasmosis."

There was that amused grin again. What was it about me that Beau found so funny?

"I'll find a place without litter boxes and get a reservation," he said. "I'll let you get back to work."

"Thanks."

He was on the verge of laughing. What the hell?

"Shelby, *relax*," he said. "You look like you think I'm about to rob you or something."

Aggravation flared in my chest. I was used to men telling me I was too uptight and needed to relax. What that really meant was that I was too uptight *for them*, and they wanted me to relax *for them*. I'd stopped dating because of the way those men made me feel, and I had no desire to be spoken to like that in my own home.

"Do you need anything else?" I asked Beau. "Because I do have work to do."

The grin slid away. "No, I'll take off now. Good luck with the work and I'll see you Monday night."

"Thanks," I said, walking over to the door to let him out and locking the dead bolt behind him.

I was ten minutes behind schedule now, but I'd work a little late to make up for it. As I sat down in my desk chair and looked out at the view of distant mountains, I took a breath and centered myself once more.

My grandparents had been the only ones to love me exactly as I was. I missed having safe people I could be myself with. One day, I'd have that again. And not only would my child be loved and cared for in all the ways my mother failed at, but they would also know that they, too, could be exactly who they were around me with no fear of judgment.

CHAPTER EIGHT

Beau

"HEY, the principal wants to see you in her office," my teammate Seth said to me as he walked into the weight room.

I finished my set of dead lifts before responding to him. "Do you know what she wants?"

He shrugged. "No, but she's on the warpath."

"Great."

Mila Pavlova was both owner and general manager of the Coyotes. She was only thirty, but she'd inherited the team from her hockey-loving father, a Russian businessman, and she knew the sport well. And while you'd think she'd earned her nickname of "Ice Queen" because she owned an ice hockey team, it had a lot more to do with her personality than anything.

"Beau," she said when I walked into her office about fifteen minutes later. "Sit down. I'm going to skip the formalities because I was expecting you about ten minutes ago."

I'd taken a quick shower before coming here because Mila had once yelled at one of my teammates for sweating all over one of the fancy chairs in her office. She was known for being impatient and having a short fuse. It wasn't just her temper that was hot, either—so was the rest of her. But every player who had ever hit on her had been shot down hard.

Personally, I wasn't into her, but she was my team owner and GM, so I had to keep her happy. Or at least, less than furious.

"I'm going to be making some moves," she said from behind her desk, tapping her bright red nails on the computer keyboard in front of her.

Shit. My luck had run out. I was going to be traded. The thought of ending up someplace like Pittsburgh made me feel sick. I needed to live near mountains and lakes, not locked up in a city.

"Relax, you're not getting traded," Mila said, finishing what she was typing and turning to face me. "But if you want to remain part of this team, I'm going to need you to step up."

"What's happening with Sergei?" I asked.

Our star defender had injured his leg in our last game, and our coaches and trainers had been tight lipped about the extent of it. This morning he'd had an appointment with a specialist, and we'd all been hoping to get some news during practice, but we hadn't.

"Out for the season," Mila said.

I hung my head. That was a blow to our entire team. Sergei was a veteran and a leader.

"Don't repeat that," she said. "Not to anyone. We're working on an announcement now. I had a feeling it was bad, which is why I'd already put some wheels in motion."

She had the same dark features as her father—long, smooth hair and big eyes. They were a dark mahogany shade that was the only warm thing about her. It was rumored that she slept at the office. Probably coiled up under her desk.

"If I'm not being traded, what do you need from me?"

"I'll be blunt, Beau." Like she was ever anything else. "You've started to look like a cardboard cutout of a hockey player."

I cleared my throat, bracing for the verbal lashing ahead.

"Our ticket sales are down, and I get why. People don't want to pay good money to come watch you guys skate up and down the ice."

"Is that all we do?" I asked with an edge.

She held a lot of control over me, but I wasn't going to sit here and listen to her bitch that my teammates and I did nothing but ice-skate.

Mila folded her hands in front of her. "It's literally all you guys do. We have the lowest average penalty minutes in the league."

"Do you want us to win? We can't score from the penalty box."

"I know that, smartass. But it's a hockey game, not a poetry reading. You guys have gotten too slick. You just execute your game and you've forgotten about the show people come here to see. They want fighting. Aggression. Heart."

She's absolutely right that we've cut down on the bullshit. Coach Maddox has drilled into us that we're here to win, not have dick-measuring contests with our opponents.

"You'd better talk to Coach about this," I said, shaking my head.

"I have. He knows about this new direction. The

thing is, you don't have to choose between winning and playing harder."

I met her gaze, well on my way to pissed. "Playing harder? Do you have any idea how hard we train to get up and down that ice as fast as we do? The game has evolved from the days you grew up watching it."

"It's not about the hockey you want to play, Beau," she said icily. "It's also about the hockey our fans pay to see. Season ticket holders who didn't renew were polled about why and they overwhelmingly said the games have gotten stale and boring."

I needed to calm down. I reminded myself that I wasn't getting traded. And that I got paid a hell of a lot of money by Mila.

"So you want us to put on more of a show," I said flatly. "More fighting."

She smiled for the first time since this meeting started. "Exactly. Chirp at your opponents. You know, tell them you wore out their mom's punch card for blow jobs."

"I know how to chirp at opponents."

Mila forged ahead, excited about the newer, more bloodthirsty approach she was forcing on us.

"I always want us to win, but I also want to see the Coyotes make the highlight reels on *SportsCenter* on game nights. I want our social media blowing up.

Furious opposing team fans in every city we visit. Some blood on the ice would be nice."

It was all I could do not to get up and storm out of her office. It was easy for her to request more blood when she wasn't the one bleeding.

"I'll see what I can do," I said.

"You're a leader on this team, Beau. You can bring up the energy level and make everyone want to play balls out. Less cuddly puppies and more cutthroat coyotes."

"Got it, boss."

"Okay, that's all," she said, going back to her computer.

I replayed our conversation as I walked back to the locker room, thinking about how I was going to tell the guys about it. But when I pushed open the locker room door, Sergei was standing there on crutches, tears streaming down his cheeks.

Out for the season. This shit sucked. And now wasn't the time to discuss what Mila had said to me.

"He's out for the season," Colby told me in a low tone. "It's bad."

I went up to Sergei and put a hand on his shoulder.

"Sorry, man," I said.

He nodded, and his anguished expression put things in perspective. Did I want to showboat and start pointless fights with my opponents? Hell no. But Sergei had it far worse than I did.

———

"Cuddly puppies?" Colby gaped at me over beers that evening at Mountain Top. "She said that?"

I nodded and took a pull from my bottle of Fat Tire.

"Jesus, she's a piece of work," Seth said.

Including me, six players had made it to this week's roundtable meeting. We got together regularly to shoot the shit, and this week I'd started things off with telling them about my conversation with Mila.

As they let off steam about our owner's new "balls out" approach, my gaze wandered over to the table I'd sat at with Shelby the night we'd met. A couple of college-aged guys were sitting there tonight, laughing, but I looked past them and remembered how intently Shelby had looked at me as she explained her dream.

I'd never met anyone as serious as she was. From what she'd told me about her parents, I knew she'd been through things kids shouldn't have to experience. My mom had taught us to approach the new kids at school, and the ones no one else paid attention to. She'd actually told us that if she found out we bullied other kids, we'd have to have her shoe surgically removed from our asses.

Shelby had probably been one of those kids. Moving from place to place and not going to school regularly. It made sense that she was serious. Life had never been carefree for her.

I'd offended her by telling her to relax the other day. I didn't mean it the way she took it, but that didn't matter. When we had dinner, I would need to tread more carefully. Show her I was someone she could relax around and be comfortable with.

"I call Jason Nestor," Colby said. "That prick is so easy to start shit with."

"No one gets to call anyone," I said. "We're all supposed to start as much shit with as many people as we can."

"It's going to be so obvious," my teammate Locke said. "I'll feel like a wrestler, faking fights and shit."

"It's only fake if both people know it," Colby said. "I'm not faking when the other guy is throwing real punches. Fuck that."

"I did hear our season ticket sales went way down this season," another teammate, Owen, said.

"Yeah?" I gave him an amused look. "Did you hear that from the chick in the front office you're banging?"

"You heard about that?"

"Everyone heard about it. You're ballsy for fucking her in her office, man."

Owen balked. "I didn't, man. I swear. We've only hooked up at her place, my place, and there was one time in my car. Who said we fucked in her office?"

"Jeremy from the sales department," Colby said. "He's the one who told me."

"That's bullshit. He's just trying to get her fired because he's an asshole."

"You should talk to someone in HR if you're dating her," I said. "If Mila finds out and she's in a mood, you never know what she'll do."

"Eh." Owen shrugged. "We're not really dating, just hooking up."

My dad had told us horror stories about seemingly innocuous decisions like banging a coworker going wrong. His life lessons were often about steering clear of legal trouble.

"It'll be your ass if she loses her job over it," I said.

"You think?"

"It could be. You're not likely to get canned. It'd be her. And she could sue. Just be careful, man."

Owen's expression sobered. The appetizers I'd ordered arrived and everyone passed plates around. I hadn't meant to bring the mood down by telling

Owen to tuck his dick back into his pants, but it needed to be said.

"I still can't believe Sergei's out," Colby said as he heaped cheese fries onto his plate. "He said the doctors are giving him a fifty percent chance of ever playing again."

"Holy shit," Seth said. "He's not even thirty yet."

"Fucking sucks," I agreed. "He doesn't deserve that shit."

"Anyone else see the irony in our owner telling us to start more fights on the same day we found out we lost our top guy to an injury?" Locke looked around the table.

Of course we saw it, but it was stupid to badmouth our owner in a public place. Instead of responding, I raised my glass.

"To Sergei. If anyone's badass enough to come back from that injury, it's him."

My teammates nodded and we toasted to our teammate. We were all quiet after that, eating and lost in our own thoughts.

Mila was right to shake things up, even if I wasn't sure she was doing it in the right way. Losing Sergei was going to change everything. He was a rock, in the locker room and on the ice.

The rest of us had to step up and try to fill a hole that couldn't possibly be filled.

CHAPTER NINE

Shelby

"DID I mention it's just dinner and I won't actually be working a pole tonight?" I asked Marlowe as I looked at my reflection while wearing the shirt she'd passed me from her closet.

She laughed. "Stop being so Victorian. It hardly even shows any cleavage."

"It's tight, though." I pulled at the side of the shirt, missing the baggy sweatshirt I'd been wearing when I arrived at her apartment.

"It's not tight; it fits you perfectly. And this is a classic. All black, three-quarter sleeves. You can do dark jeans and heels, flats, or booties."

"Flats."

"What colors do you have? Red would be fun."

I turned from the mirror and met her gaze. "I have black and dark gray."

"Of course you do." She rolled her eyes. "What's your shoe size?"

"Eight."

"Damn, I'm a six or I'd loan you shoes, too."

I gave her a pointed look. "You're smaller than me, which is why the shirt doesn't fit, either."

"Cut the shit. It looks perfect. That top is too big for me anyways. Just keep it after you peel it off Beau's bedroom floor in the morning."

I laughed hard at that. "This is just a friendly dinner."

"Oh, young Padawan. There are no friendly dinners. He wants to pet the kitty."

I gave my friend a skeptical look. "Beau Fox has a wide variety of kitties to choose from. And he knows I want to keep our arrangement all business."

"Uh-huh." She walked into the bathroom, still talking. "Why are you fighting it, Shelby? There are worse men to have a fling with. He's hot and you know he's experienced in bed."

I wrinkled my nose at the thought, because I wasn't someone who could have casual sex. Or at least, I couldn't enjoy it. And who wanted to be a man's 113th partner? Definitely not me.

"Get in here so I can do your hair!" Marlowe yelled from the bathroom.

I took a final look at the shirt, which I was apparently wearing to dinner, and walked into the bathroom.

"It's still wet," I said.

"That's why I'm going to dry it." She arched a brow.

"Don't be so salty. I'm not into hairstyling."

Marlowe smiled. "Just sit down and let me work my magic."

"Okay, but don't make it fancy. I don't want it to look like I'm trying to make it into a date."

I sat down and Marlowe, standing behind me, met my gaze in the mirror. "Anything other than sweats and a ponytail is fancy to you."

"I like being comfortable, okay? I'm not used to wearing shirts that make me look like I painted my chest black."

"You're pretty, Shelby. Why do you try so hard to make yourself look average when you're so pretty?"

My gaze instinctively shot to my lap as a long-forgotten childhood memory came rushing back.

My mother held my upper arm, squeezing it as she practically dragged me out the front door of the restaurant we'd met her latest boyfriend at for dinner.

Our coats were still inside, and the winter air stung my cheeks. She finally let go of my arm, glaring at me.

"You are not ruining this for me, Shelby. Tony is my boyfriend. I expect you to smile at him and look interested in what he's saying."

I was eleven, and I didn't like Tony. He talked nonstop about what a big deal he was and how scared his employees were of him firing them. I was embarrassed for my mom, who was heavily made up and wearing a tight, low-cut leopard-print shirt.

"I want to go home," I said.

My mom bent down, her eyes narrowed. "Smile and laugh when I do. If you fuck up one more time, I'm throwing away your library books and you can forget about getting a ride to school anymore. Are we clear?"

Throwing away my library books would mean I could never check out more. She meant it, too. The only thing my mom took seriously was flirting with men. They were her only source of income, after all.

"Yes," I said, tears welling in my eyes. "We're clear."

"Shelby, are you okay?" Marlowe asked, giving my shoulder a small shake.

"It's because of my mom," I said, answering her earlier question. "When I was a kid, she dressed up and went out to bars trying to land men. It's actually a lot more screwed up than that, but…I probably try too hard to not be like her."

"Well, shit." Marlowe bent her knees and threw her arms around my neck, hugging me from behind. "I'm an asshole. I'm sorry, Shelby."

"I wasn't trying to make you feel sorry for me. I was just being honest."

"I know." She stood up and reached for her blow-dryer. "And you're nothing like her, I promise. I just want you to look and feel like the beautiful woman you are."

I scoffed. "I'm average on a good day, but you're a true friend for saying that."

"Wait and see when I'm done."

An hour later, I marveled at the transformation she'd managed. My makeup was natural, but it brought out my features in ways I never imagined. Marlowe had styled my hair in loose waves I couldn't help running my fingers through.

"Wow, I can't believe this is me," I said, turning from side to side to admire my reflection.

"If Beau doesn't immediately tell you you're beautiful, walk right back out of that restaurant," she said. "I don't have plans tonight, so we can watch a movie and order pizza."

"Oh, don't tempt me. I'm going into an uncomfortable situation, so you know I'll be looking for any excuse to bail."

"SHELBY, WOW. I MEAN…WOW."

It was less than an hour after my conversation with Marlowe, and Beau was standing outside my apartment door getting his first look at the made-over me.

"My friend likes doing hair and makeup," I explained, sifting through my bag for the lipstick I already knew was there.

"Well, you look amazing."

I looked up from my bag, smiling at him. How could I not? He was easy on the eyes, he'd paid me a nice compliment, and I'd just realized that as of yesterday morning, my period was late.

How had I forgotten? Getting pregnant consumed my thoughts, but I hadn't looked at my period tracker for several days. It was too early to share my hopes out loud with anyone, but I was still giddy.

"Thank you," I said, excitement swirling in my stomach.

"Ready to go?"

"I am."

I grabbed my coat, closed and locked my apartment door, then walked beside him to his car, which turned out to be a dark gray Range Rover.

"My winter chariot," he said as he opened my door, adding, "I like the boots."

There was snow on the ground, so I'd worn my insulated winter boots instead of the flats Marlowe recommended.

"Thanks."

He'd picked me up for dinner instead of meeting me and complimented me twice. I had a nervous twinge that made me give him a skeptical look.

"What?" he asked.

"This is just a friendly dinner, right?" I clarified. "We're doing separate checks and like…fist-bumping at the end?"

He laughed, bringing out the laugh lines that were probably my favorite of his features.

"I've never met anyone like you, Shelby."

What did that mean, though? Did he see me as a challenge because I was more neurotic and less glitzy than the women he was used to? Because that didn't even make sense. I had to credit Beau with one thing—I definitely couldn't figure him out.

"Yeah, we can fist-bump if you want," he said. "And no, I'm not trying to get you into bed. Unless you want me to."

Ugh, how cringeworthy would that be?

"No, I don't want that. I mean, no offense. You're great, but I'm done with dating."

"Done?" He glanced over at me as he stopped at a light.

"Yeah, I tried for years. And now that I can hopefully have a baby all on my own, I don't need a man."

"But do you ever *want* one? If you don't mind me asking."

All the awful first dates flooded through my mind. Once I filtered out the unstable men and the ones only looking for sex, there weren't many left. And if they were somebody I could see myself with, the feeling was never mutual. It was a roller coaster of rising and falling hopes, and it had felt good to just step onto level ground again by deciding not to do it anymore.

"Honestly, no," I said. "You said you've never met anyone like me, and I think the men I went out with would agree. I know who I am, and I know it's not what most men want. Or maybe any men. I'm uptight and set in my ways. For a long time, I tried to change and be like other women. But finally, I decided I'm happy just being myself. *I* like me. That's all that really matters."

As he pulled into the parking lot of a steakhouse, Beau said, "I admire that. And when I said you're not like anyone I've ever met, I didn't mean it in a bad way. I like that about you."

I had no idea how to respond to that, so I went

with the safe choice and said nothing. Beau parked the car and met my gaze, then looked at his watch.

"I made a reservation and we're right on time. And I'll make you a deal."

"A deal?"

"I won't put the moves on you, but I am paying the check tonight. I asked you to dinner and that's what I do anytime I ask a friend to dinner."

"Are we friends?"

He grinned. "I hope so."

I nodded. "Okay."

The restaurant was a local favorite, a small crowd gathered around the waiting area. Since we had a reservation, we were led to our table right away.

"Beau Fox," someone said as we passed them. "Dude, I think that's Beau Fox from the Coyotes."

Beau turned and gave him a quick smile and nod. What was that like, having people recognize you in public?

Our table for two was tucked into a corner of the restaurant, the walls nearby adorned with old news clippings about Denver's history. Beau immediately ordered a basket of the restaurant's rolls and the whipped cinnamon butter they were known for.

"So you've never been here?" he asked.

I shook my head. "I mostly cook for myself or DoorDash."

"I think you'll like it. Their steaks are phenomenal."

He was right about the rolls. They melted in my mouth and I was considering a second one when he sat back in his seat, elbows on the table as he seemed to study me.

"You said you moved around a lot as a kid," he said. "Before you moved in with your grandparents. Was there any place you liked best?"

I answered immediately. "Chicago. We lived in an apartment above a Laundromat and a martial arts studio when I was twelve. My mom…well, I already told you she's bipolar. She would have episodes sometimes where she locked me out of the apartment. Sometimes it lasted several days. The owner of the martial arts place saw me sitting at the top of the stairway one of those times, because I had nowhere else to go. His name was Doug. He asked if he could hire me to clean his studio in exchange for meals and free self-defense lessons."

"Sounds like a good guy to have in your corner," Beau said.

"The best." My throat tightened as I remembered his kindness. "And he made it sound like he needed my help, but really all I did was sweep the floor. He made me feel important for the first time in my life.

That was the hardest place for me to leave when my mom fell behind and couldn't pay rent anymore."

"Do you still remember the self-defense skills you learned?"

I smiled. "All of it. Doug stayed after classes to work with me and make sure I could defend myself. I think he knew I'd need it."

Beau's brow furrowed. "Nothing serious, I hope."

I shrugged. "We lived in some rough neighborhoods, and my mom brought home some questionable characters."

"Damn."

"When was your first fight?" I asked him, eager to have the spotlight shining on him instead of me.

He laughed. "My brothers and I fought all the time. Since I was in the middle, both of them fought with me but not so much with each other. But my first fight with someone else…let's see…I guess I was about nine. A teammate and I got into it after a game."

"Nine?" My eyes widened. "Did you guys get in trouble?"

He shook his head, looking dismissive. "Fighting is part of hockey. You get used to it."

"Do you still have all your teeth?"

He grinned. "One of my front teeth got chipped

in a high school game, so I've got a filling. Other than that, they're all mine."

He told me about life as a pro hockey player and I told him about working my way through law school as a waitress, tutor, and library clerk. He ate a massive steak, baked potato, and a salad, and I had spicy chicken pasta. The time flew by quickly and before I knew it, a few hours had already passed.

"I should probably get home," I said. "I have to be up early for work in the morning."

"Yeah, me too."

He drove me home and I realized on the way that I hadn't thought about whether I might be pregnant all evening. Our laughs and conversation had taken my mind off it.

"I had a nice time," I said as Beau parked in front of my building.

"Me too. We should hang out again soon."

"Sure."

He got out of his car and walked up to my door with me, where he waited for me to unlock it and then smiled and held out a closed fist.

I laughed and gave him the fist bump I'd mentioned earlier.

"Night, Shelby," he said as I walked inside.

"Good night."

CHAPTER TEN

Beau

SHELBY: Can you stop by sometime? I have something for you.

I'd already read the text many times today, and I'd responded to it as soon as I stepped off the plane in Calgary this morning, where I'd played a game tonight. Still, it intrigued me.

What could she have for me? Part of me hoped she'd warmed to me after our dinner earlier this week, but part of me didn't.

I'd *seen* Shelby that night. Really seen her, for the first time. Before, I'd known she was a strong, resilient woman who had been through some shit.

But some of the things she said the night we had dinner had stayed with me.

Men not liking who she was. Learning self-defense because her home wasn't safe. And she hadn't had even one parent to rely on for most of her childhood.

"Fox, get your shoulder back in the ice," our team trainer Chris said. "Five more minutes."

I nodded and sat my phone on the chair next to the ice tub in the Calgary visitors' locker room. It was boring just sitting here, but I had to because I'd taken a hard hit to my right shoulder in the game.

Mila had gotten what she'd wanted. I'd trash-talked my way into two fights tonight, and I was sore as shit. We'd won the game, but we were a different team without Sergei. Mila had been right about that.

"Want one?" Colby held up something wrapped in white paper that looked like a sub sandwich.

"Yeah." I went to grab it with my right arm but cringed and froze from the pain in my shoulder.

"Here you go, princess," Colby said, moving the sandwich just a couple of inches from my left hand so I could easily get it. "You want me to cut it into bites for you? Make some airplane sounds and feed it to you?"

"Just give me the sandwich and fuck off."

He did, and I set the sandwich on the chair where

my phone was. I was starving. My shifts on the ice tonight had been long. I ungracefully managed to unwrap the sandwich, which turned out to be a meatball sub—my favorite.

"Fox, get your shoulder back in the ice!" Chris called from across the room.

I submerged myself into the freezing ice and water, just my head and left arm above the surface so I could eat. Shelby's text returned to the front of my mind.

I'd stop by as soon as I got home from my road trip, and I wanted us to remain friends, but I'd decided not to pursue anything more with her. She was too good for that. Just because I found her intriguing, that didn't make it right to try to charm my way into her bed.

She'd told me clearly that she didn't want to be more than friends, and I would respect that. Just friends with the woman who was having my kid. I knew it was for the best, though.

Shelby deserved to find an amazing man and be treated like a queen one day. I wouldn't be that man, though.

———

"Hi!" Shelby beamed at me as she opened her apartment door. "Come in!"

I stomped the snow from my boots on the mat next to her door and crouched down to untie them.

"How was your trip?" she asked.

I looked up at her. "It's colder there than here. But we won."

"That's great!"

Once my shoes were off, I stood up and our eyes met. She had little, if any makeup on, and her hair was up in a messy bun. Still, she was pretty. For the first time, I had a friend I found attractive.

"So I have news," she said, her eyes sparkling. "I'm pregnant."

"What?" I grinned and opened my arms to hug her. "That's amazing. Congratulations!"

"Thanks!" She hugged me and I picked up on a sweet scent that reminded me of a bakery. "Only you and Marlowe know, and it was so hard to wait until you got back to tell you."

Wow. The news was hitting differently than I'd expected it to. Shelby was having my kid. Even though it wouldn't be my kid to care for, biologically it was mine. I'd thought I'd feel like Santa Claus, giving someone an amazing gift and then peacing out on my sleigh.

Instead, I felt...weird. I couldn't ruin Shelby's moment by saying so, though.

"How far along?" I asked her.

"Almost six weeks."

"And how are you feeling?"

She burst into a huge smile. "I've never been so happy. I can't believe it worked on the first try. You must have potent sperm."

"Yeah, my brother got his wife pregnant immediately both times they tried. I guess it was three times, actually. They lost one early on."

Shelby put her hand on her stomach, which was still flat. "I kind of want to wrap myself in Bubble Wrap and never leave the apartment. I know miscarriages happen, and it's not because of anything the mother did wrong, but it's hard not to worry."

"This is a time for celebrating, not worrying."

Her expression lit up. "Which reminds me. I said I had something for you."

She walked into the kitchen and took a white box from the table, bringing it to me.

"I made hot cross buns. To celebrate my bun in the oven. And also, cinnamon rolls."

I grinned. "This explains why you smell so good."

"I do?"

"Yeah, kind of like vanilla and cinnamon."

Good enough to eat, I would have added with a

wicked grin if she were any other woman I was this attracted to. Not Shelby, though. I wasn't as emotionally checked out about her baby as I'd expected to be, and I needed to stay on good terms with her for at least the next couple of decades. Maybe I'd want to play a small role in my child's life, if she'd let me. Even if the kid only knew me as her friend.

"I just want to go buy all the baby things," she said, sighing wistfully. "I know I should wait, but I don't think I can."

"I'll take you shopping."

It was a terrible idea, but the offer popped out before I had time to think it through. There was a back and forth in my head between what I wanted and what was best.

"I'd take you up on that, but Marlowe and I are going shopping on Tuesday. She's flying out Wednesday for the long weekend."

"That's right, Thanksgiving. Do you have plans?"

There was a flash of something in her eyes, but she covered it quickly with a smile.

"I'm taking the day off and reorganizing my closets. I'll make soup or something. I'm not big on turkey."

My parents hosted a huge Fox family Thanksgiving every year. With aunts, uncles, and cousins, we usually had at least twenty-five people, some-times more. There was always way too much food and alcohol, football, and board games.

"Why don't you come to my parents' house with me for Thanksgiving?" I asked. "My mom puts on a big spread. It's always a good time."

"Oh no, I'm good. I'm used to spending holidays on my own. I don't mind it at all."

I couldn't stand the thought of her cleaning out closets by herself on Thanksgiving. My family was used to me bringing teammates to holiday gather-ings because they didn't have family close by. One year, I'd brought five teammates who had put away four entire pies.

"I'll pick you up at ten that morning if that works," I told Shelby.

She lowered her brows. "No, I'm eating soup in my kitchen."

"No, you're coming with me."

She scoffed. "Don't be that guy, Beau. I don't want to go to a big family thing with people I don't know. I'd be super uncomfortable. Remember what I said—I know I'm not like other people, but I like me."

I had to tread carefully, because I could tell from her tone she was getting pissed. But I wasn't backing down.

"I like you, too, and so will my family. I wouldn't take you to something you'd be uncomfortable at."

"Look, I appreciate the offer, but no. Now I need to get back to work, so enjoy the baked goods and"

"And I'll see you Thursday morning. We're casual people. I'll be wearing jeans and a flannel."

"Beau." She glared at me, the swirling greens and brows in her eyes reminding me of a forest, though they were anything but peaceful at this moment.

"Shelby."

She shrugged. "Fine, I just won't open the door."

"Fine, I'll sit outside until you open the door and miss Thanksgiving. Hope you'll at least share your soup with me."

She sighed dramatically. "Why are you being like this?"

"Why are *you* being like this?"

"I don't want to be exposed to germs during flu season. But thanks for thinking of me."

I shook my head. "My sister's pregnant and she'll be there. I promise no one will get in your face."

"I just don't want to go," she said, exasperated.

"And I just don't want you here by yourself on Thanksgiving."

She narrowed her eyes. "I am not your charity case, Beau Fox. If you show up at Thanksgiving lunch, or dinner, or whatever, with a woman, your family will think we're together."

I considered. "Maybe. But who cares? Just don't mention that you're pregnant. That's a minefield we don't want to walk onto."

"You're right, it could be uncomfortable. So I'm not going."

"I'll be here at ten. You don't need to bring anything. My mom cooks most of the food but has some of it catered. You're eating for two now, so it'd be best for the baby if you came and had a good meal."

"I can eat a good meal here." She gave me a death glare.

"I'll see you Thursday."

"Beau…" She shook her head and looked away.

"Hey," I said, sensing her rising anxiety. "Trust me, okay?"

She said nothing, which was better than biting back with another argument.

"Thanks for these," I said, nodding at the box. "And congratulations again."

"Go away," she said, but there was a lot less fire in her tone now.

"Bye, Shelby," I said with a grin.

"Bye, you stubborn asshole."

CHAPTER ELEVEN

Shelby

"You grew up here?" I asked Beau, stunned as his parents' home came into view at the end of a long, private driveway.

It was a sprawling log home on a lake with stone pillars and huge windows, and no other homes in sight. I'd seen homes like this one in architecture magazines. This notched the intimidation factor up even further. While I'd known his parents likely had a beautiful home, I hadn't expected *this*.

"No, they built this about ten years ago. I grew up in a house in a subdivision in the city."

"This is incredible," I said as he parked on one side of a large portico.

"They've got about fifty acres. In the summer, we fish and ride four wheelers and in the winter, we ice-skate on the lake when it freezes over."

I shuddered. "I could never ice-skate on a lake."

He grinned. "Sure you could."

"Worrying about falling through the ice would ruin it."

He gave me an amused look. "Ready to meet the den?"

"I see what you did there. Because you guys are the Foxes."

He winked, and I said a last-minute prayer that the rest of the family was as easy to be around as he was.

"Let's come up with a signal," I said as we approached the wooden front doors. "If I say anything about peppermint tea, it means I want to leave immediately."

He gave me a look. "Can we at least eat first?"

"Depends how uncomfortable I am. Remember whose idea this was?"

"Oh, nice," he muttered. "They're a subtle bunch."

I followed his gaze to a window, where several faces were crowded around each other looking at us.

"Why are they staring at me?" I gave him a panicked look. "I hate this already."

"It's fine. They're just a little excited because I've never brought a woman to a family thing."

I turned to him, my heart racing as his words sank in. "But this isn't"

The front door opened then and we were greeted by a woman I assumed was his mother. "You must be Shelby." She was a pretty woman with a choppy silver bob. She reached out to hug me as she introduced herself. "I'm Claire. We're so thrilled you're here. Come in, come in. Can I take your coat?"

As I took off my coat, I took in my surroundings. The inside of the house was just as beautiful as the outside. It was two stories of wide-open space, bright with natural light from the many windows and decorated in a modern rustic style. My gaze stopped on a cluster of people standing about fifteen feet away, some with faces I recognized from the window.

A pretty woman with long, dark hair lunged toward me first.

"Hi, I'm Fiona. Should I take you directly to Beau's embarrassing childhood photos or do you want to grab a drink first?"

She reminded me of Marlowe. I liked her immediately.

"Hey," Beau said, waving. "Anyone planning to acknowledge me?"

A tall, handsome man who looked a lot like Beau scoffed as he approached me. "We've been acknowledging you your entire life, you diva. We want to talk to Shelby. I'm Asher, by the way. Beau's wiser, older brother."

It was a whirlwind of introductions. I met his younger siblings, Isaac and Genevieve, Fiona's husband Adrian, Asher's wife Claire and their children Anderson and Amara, his paternal grandma, Sophia, his Aunt Gabrielle and Uncle Steve, and finally, his dad, Henry.

"Do you work, Shelby?" Claire asked as I stood in the kitchen between her and her husband. "Or are you still in school?"

"I'm an attorney."

Henry grinned, an older version of his son, and put a hand on my shoulder. "Finally, someone I can talk shop with. What sort of law do you practice?"

"I own my own legal research business."

He nodded, looking impressed. "Do you specialize in anything, or just take the cases that interest you most?"

I shrugged. "A little of both, actually. I took a break from corporate bankruptcy because I like being able to stay awake until the end of the workday."

He chuckled, his eyes sparkling as he looked at his wife. "I like her."

"I think we all do," Claire said. "We're so glad you joined us, Shelby. I'm sorry I can't spend more time getting to know you since I'm busy in the kitchen, but I hope we can sit down later and chat."

She was so warm and welcoming. My instinct was to sit down, try to blend in, and say as little as possible, but Claire made me want to try something else.

"Can I help in the kitchen?" I asked her.

"She's way better than the help you're used to," Beau said. "She made the most amazing homemade cinnamon rolls the other day."

Fiona's expression turned dreamy. "Oh my god, the baby has been craving cinnamon rolls. I'll have to get the recipe from you."

Isaac cringed. "Or not. Remember when you started an oven fire?"

She rolled her eyes. "Like any of you will ever let me forget it. That was more than a decade ago."

Genevieve laughed. "Right, but wasn't it…just last Thanksgiving when you made those god-awful mashed potatoes?"

Everyone groaned.

"They were like porridge," Asher said. "Not even gravy could help."

"You guys, how was I supposed to know you can only make mashed potatoes with certain kinds of potatoes? I thought a potato was a potato," Fiona said, sitting down and opening a can of seltzer water.

"And that's why we're on a first-name basis with so many Uber Eats drivers," Adrian said.

Beau, Asher, Genevieve, and Isaac ignored his comment. I got the impression it was okay with them that they make fun of their sister, but they didn't think her husband should jump on the bandwagon.

"What can I help with?" I asked Claire.

"If you're sure you want to help, I have ten pounds of potatoes that need to be peeled."

"Sure, Beau and I will do that."

Beau arched a brow at me, amused. "We will?"

"Yep."

Isaac made a whip-cracking sound and Beau gave him the finger. I passed Beau a knife and took another one from the block on the island for myself.

Potatoes were a safe bet. I'd noticed that smelling and looking at certain foods made me feel sick, sometimes to the point I didn't even want to eat anymore.

"So Shelby, how did you and Beau meet?" Claire asked as she stirred something on the stove.

I met Beau's gaze, wide eyed. We should have gotten our story straight before this. I couldn't exactly tell them about the binder and my efforts to help him jerk off into a cup.

"We met at Mountain Top after one of my games," he said. "She saw me signing the tits of the Foxes and knew I was something special."

"Oh, Beau," his mom said disapprovingly. "You're still doing that?"

He shrugged and grinned playfully. "They ask me to, Mom."

"I recall teaching you the word *no*."

"They're all your age or older. I'm not getting my rocks off, trust me."

Asher snorted from the living room, which was open to the kitchen. "I bet they are, though. Beau's making their old lady bits tingly."

"Boys," Henry said, giving Asher a disapproving look over the rim of his dark-framed glasses. "Can we not be so lewd when we have company?"

"Daddy, what's old lady bits?" Anderson asked Asher.

Asher looked at his wife, who shook her head and said, "Don't look at me. That's all you."

"You're not old enough for the answer to that question yet," Asher said.

Isaac intervened. "You guys shouldn't teach them that anything is too shameful to talk about."

"That's right!" Claire answered from the stove.

Asher gave his son an excited look. "Hey buddy, want to build a Lego castle?"

"Yeah! Let's go!"

Anderson took his dad's hand and ran up the open staircase to the second level of the house, where the Legos apparently were.

"We're master deflectors," Chloe said.

"Doing okay?" Beau asked me under his breath.

I nodded and smiled, because…I was. His family was as easygoing as he was. I thought about the growing life inside me and wished he or she could have a family like this. People to be with on holidays. Siblings who knew each other's funny stories. My child wouldn't have anyone but me.

Would I be enough? No matter what I did, I couldn't give my child a big family. It hadn't seemed like a big deal until now.

"Hey," Beau said softly, looking confused. "Peppermint tea?"

"Oh…" I relaxed my expression, which had probably been looking worried. "No, I'm good."

"Try this," Fiona said, holding a cracker with dip on it in front of Beau's mouth since his hands were occupied with potato peeling.

He opened his mouth and let her push it past his lips.

"Mm, that's good," he said.

"Right? It's everything dip. Mom ordered it from the caterers. I'm obsessed with it."

"You should try it," he said to me.

"I will."

Fiona dipped another cracker and held it up to my mouth. I opened and she popped it in. And she was right—it was creamy and garlicky and delicious.

"Don't you just want to eat it with a spoon?" she asked. "Or is that just me because I'm pregnant?"

Beau shook his head. "Nah, you were a weirdo before you were pregnant, too."

"I just realized none of your teammates came this year," Henry said from the living room. "I can't remember you ever coming to Thanksgiving without teammates."

"Coach had all the orphans over to his house this year," Beau said. "But Dalton asked me to bring him a piece of Mom's pecan pie."

"He's such a sweetheart," Claire said.

Beau shook his head at me and spoke in a low tone. "He's got my mom wrapped around his little finger."

We peeled potatoes and Beau put them on the stove in a big pot of water to boil. I kept busy for the next hour helping in the kitchen and then everyone sat down to dinner at Henry and Claire's long solid wood dining table.

I hadn't felt so much like a part of a family since my grandparents were alive. But I had to remind myself I was only part of the Fox family for today. Then I'd go back to being a lone wolf.

"Shelby, how do you feel about Scrabble?" Genevieve asked me after the meal.

It was a Fox family tradition that the men cleaned up after the meal on holidays. The women were all relaxing in the living room, some with a glass of wine in hand. I had a mug of warm apple cider.

"I think it's the most underrated board game out there," I told Beau's younger sister.

"So you're a fan?" she asked brightly.

"Don't do it, Shelby," Fiona said from the recliner she was stretched out in. "She's a supernerd. She plays Scrabble on weekends for funsies."

"Me too, when I can find someone to play with," I said.

The truth? I played it on my phone, because I had no one to play against in real life. I wasn't going to mention that, though.

"Let's play," Genevieve said, getting up from her seat. "Mom, you'll play, right?"

"Of course."

"Chloe?"

Chloe shook her head. "No thanks. I'm going to watch the game."

Fiona was right. Genevieve was good. We played three games and she took two of them. I won the last one, though, winning by more than fifty points. And I never felt self-conscious or awkward, even with Beau all the way in the living room watching football.

It was evening when we left, and I was exhausted, full of pie and happier than I'd been in a long time. Beau's family was even better than I'd imagined them when I was researching him.

"Better than organizing your closets?" he asked me on the drive back to my apartment.

"Yes. I had a great time. Thanks for inviting me."

"Anytime."

I couldn't go back anytime, though. Once my pregnancy started showing, there would be questions. I tried not to think that far ahead, though.

Today had been great. That was enough.

CHAPTER TWELVE

Beau

"BEAU, I'M A VIRGIN."

Shelby stood next to a bed, wearing sheer white lingerie with thin straps that fell almost to her knees. She slid her fingers beneath the straps and it fell to the floor, revealing her flawless skin and the supple curves of her body.

"Teach me," she said, running a hand down her stomach. "Teach me how to make you crazy."

I was crazy already, aching to get my hands on her. What would I do first? Her breasts called out to be cupped and kissed and her nipples begged to be teased and sucked.

Her first. I was going to be her first, and her only. I

was so turned on just looking at her. Shelby had never shared this part of herself with anyone; it was all mine.

"Touch me," she said, stepping closer to the bed. "Please."

I SHIFTED AROUND IN BED, belatedly realizing I was rock hard. And I knew whyI'd been dreaming about Shelby again.

As I'd fallen asleep in my Chicago hotel room last night, I'd imagined I was hunting a bear, hoping I'd dream about that. But instead, I'd fantasized about the woman I was trying my best not to think of in a sexual way.

She was ten weeks along now, and we texted daily but hadn't been able to see much of each other since Thanksgiving due to our schedules. Shelby treated her working hours like she was in an office; she wouldn't blow off work to hang out if I was free during the week. And she was working extra hours in the evenings to catch up on research for a case that had an earlier trial date than originally expected.

I'd met a woman in a bar last night after the game. Alyssa. She was hot, but I wasn't feeling anything more than some light flirting. At some point, I'd grown fond of Shelby's resistance to my charms. I'd never been with a woman like her, who challenged me and didn't get stars in her eyes every time I spoke.

Though I'd always thought I liked women who fell into bed easily, the only woman on my mind was the one who wanted nothing to do with me between the sheets.

Fuck. How had I gotten myself into this mess?

I pushed the bedcovers aside and got to work. Morning wood was part of my daily life now, and my routine was fantasizing about Shelby riding my dick until she screamed with pleasure.

Closing my eyes, I pictured her letting loose, showing me a side of her no one had ever seen before. It didn't take long for me to finish and grab a tissue from the bedside table to clean up with.

I showered, dressed, and packed my bag. The team had a flight to Las Vegas in a couple of hours, so I had enough time to drop my bag off at the front desk, get breakfast at the hotel restaurant, and board the bus we'd take to the airport on time.

When I sat down across from Dalton in the restaurant, he looked up at me and nodded.

"Sup?"

He had a black eye I didn't remember seeing in the locker room after the game. I lowered my brows, trying to figure out if I'd missed something.

"Got into it with some drunk guys at a bar last night," he said. "Chicago fans."

"Shit, man. You okay?"

He scoffed. "Yeah, I'm fine. Those assholes called the cops but the cops asked to see the surveillance video from the bar and they ended up arresting the douchebag fans who called them. Colby and I got a little banged up, but it was worth it."

"Chicago fans are fucking nuts."

He nodded in the direction of the breakfast bar. "Go get some of that sausage while they still have some. It's really good."

I considered a joke about him liking sausage, but nah. He'd had a rough night.

When I got back to the table, Colby was there, too, and he was giving me a funny look.

"What?" I asked.

"You got some pop-up on your phone about your baby being the size of an apricot. Didn't know you had a uterus, bro."

Shit. I'd subscribed to some shit about fetal development and since I'd input Shelby's due date, they kept sending me updates about what was going on that week during her pregnancy.

"My sister's pregnant," I said, glad for the out. "I like to keep up with the development of the baby."

Fiona was five months along, but my teammates didn't know that.

"An apricot?" Dalton shook his head. "That's a weird thing to compare it to."

"Yeah, people eat apricots," Colby said. "They should be more sensitive. Compare it to like, an egg or something."

"People eat eggs too, dumbass," I said.

"Oh, yeah. Sorry, long night."

I looked closer at his face. He had a fat lip and a cut on his cheek.

"Heard you got your ass kicked last night," I said.

With a single note of laughter, he touched his cheek near the cut. "Yeah. Like I didn't get enough on the ice."

The increase in fighting during games was why I'd gone back to the hotel instead of out with my teammates last night. These days I was beat after every game—literally. My shoulder still hadn't healed all the way and I was sore all over.

"I mean, we kind of deserved it," Colby said, grinning. "We were assholes to Petrov last night."

Chicago's team captain had broad enough shoulders to take the chirping, but his fans were apparently offended on his behalf.

Other teammates started showing up to eat at the restaurant. I finished off one plate before filling another one, then checked my phone while I waited for everyone else to finish.

No *good morning, great game last night* text from Shelby, of course. Anytime I'd started any sort of communication with other women, they'd immediately started the good morning and good night texts. I hated them. If someone was in a relationship, that was one thing, but when you'd just hooked up once or not at all? Too much.

It would've been nice to get one occasionally from Shelby, though. She literally didn't want me at all, and it frustrated and amused me in equal measure.

Maybe not so equal. I was becoming more frustrated than amused, especially since my only sexual partner in the past two months was my hand.

I texted her instead.

Me: Hey, good morning from Chi town. How are you feeling?

She'd been experiencing morning sickness, and sometimes it stretched into the rest of the day, too.

Shelby: Like crap. I'm working in bed with a bucket beside me.

Me: Are you keeping any food down?

Shelby: Not much. My doctor said to come in if I can't keep water down today.

Me: Are you able to drive?

Shelby: I could if I had to. Or Marlowe could take me.

Me: I'm flying to Vegas soon. I'll check on you after I land.

Shelby: You don't have to. I'll go to the doctor if I get worse.

Me: I'll check on you.

Shelby: Okay. Thanks.

Me: Hope you feel better.

I googled ideas to help with morning sickness and saw that ginger was high on a couple of lists. Surely even Shelby, who was paranoid about everything that went into her body while she was pregnant, would eat ginger.

There was a great local bakery in Denver that my mom ordered from all the time. I left my table in the restaurant and found an empty hallway where I could get some privacy and dialed the number I'd found online.

"Judy's, how can I help you?" the voice on the other end of the line said.

"Hey, this is Beau Fox. My mom, Claire Fox, is a regular customer."

"Oh, of course. We just took her order for Christmas. What can I do for you?"

"I need to order some ginger cookies to be delivered to someone in Denver."

There was a pause on the other end of the line. "Ginger cookies?"

"Right."

"We could do gingerbread men, how about that?"

"As long as they have ginger."

"They do."

I gave her Shelby's address and my credit card number. Hopefully the cookies would help. They were the least I could do from several states away.

———

"HEY, ARE YOU FEELING BETTER?" I asked Shelby several hours later.

We'd gone from the airport to the Las Vegas arena for our pregame skate, and I was calling her from the visitors' locker room.

"Maybe a tiny bit," she said. "But I'm so tired, I could fall asleep right this second."

"Are you keeping water down?"

"Yes," she said, sounding amused. "I've got you, Marlowe, and a nurse from my doctor's office asking me how often I'm throwing up."

"Try Gatorade," I suggested.

"I've got one on my nightstand now. Marlowe brought over a bunch earlier this afternoon."

"Okay, good."

"How's Vegas?"

"Decent weather," I said. "Other than that, it's same old, same old."

"But more strippers, right? More than Denver, at least."

"Hmm, I guess so. Not really my thing, though."

She sighed softly. "Sorry, I'm grouchy."

"You're entitled." I suddenly remembered why I'd called instead of texting. "Hey, I want you to come to my parents' house for Christmas with me."

There was a pause on the other end of the line before she said, "I don't think I can, Beau."

"Of course you can. I don't think I'm even invited unless you're with me. Just about every member of my family has called or texted in the last week telling me to bring you. Especially my dad. He can't wait to talk shop again."

There was a smile in her tone. "That's so nice of them. But I'm so sick and I'd either look like a jerk who came to a gathering while I'm sick or a pregnant woman, and I don't like either option."

Shit. I'd forgotten how sick she was. She had a point, but it didn't feel right for her to be alone on Christmas.

"I'll be fine. Don't you worry about me," she said, seeming to read my mind. "I'm taking Christmas Eve and Christmas off and honestly, I'm planning to lie on my couch, catch up on shows, and sleep."

"You could wear a mask," I said. "My family really wants you to come."

That was true, but what I really meant and couldn't bring myself to say was *I really want you to come.*

"If I wasn't sick and completely exhausted, I'd be there. I love your family. Maybe I'll get lucky and be better by next week. But if not, I need to stay home."

"Okay, well h"

"Hang on, there's someone at my door. That's weird, because Marlowe is the only person it could be and she always texts first. Ugh, getting out of bed is the worst." There was a pause. "It looks like a delivery person. Okay, I'm going to open the door. Stay on the line and call the police if you hear me being murdered."

"Jesus, Shelby."

"Hey, thank you so much. Let me grab my purse and tip you…oh, really? Okay, well, thank you."

I heard her close and lock the door and then she returned to our call.

"It's from a bakery," she said, sounding confused. "I bet they got the address wrong. I should go grab the delivery guy so he can take it back. Hang on a sec."

"Hey, wait. They didn't get the address wrong."

"I just saw the note on top. *Feel better soon—Beau.* That was so nice of you, thank you. And you even tipped the delivery guy."

I smiled, because it was the first time in a while I'd heard her sound so happy.

"They're ginger cookies. Ginger helps"

"With morning sickness," she finished for me. "Thank you. These look and smell amazing. I'm going to try one right now."

I waited a few seconds.

"Oh wow, these are amazing. They're ginger-bread men, but they're soft and they have actual frosting instead of just little lines of decoration icing."

"I'm glad you like them."

Everyone in the locker room was gathering by the whiteboard for a meeting with our coaches.

"Hey, I have to go," I said. "I'll talk to you later. Eat the cookies and drink the Gatorade. And fuck work. It can wait. You need to rest."

She gave a wistful little moan. "Maybe I will. I can always work later."

"Text me later, okay?"

"I will."

CHAPTER THIRTEEN

Shelby

I RAN my fingers over the worn album cover of the most treasured record in my collection. When I'd lived with my grandparents, my grandpa always played this collection of classic Christmas music as we decorated the tree he cut down from a local tree farm.

Now I had his prized vintage record player and I played this album once a year, on Christmas. Memories of holidays with my grandparents brought a hollow feeling to my chest every time I thought of them, so I could only listen to it one time, in their memory, and then I always tucked it back into its sleeve until next year.

I'd been honest with Beau—I was too sick to go with him to his parents' house for Christmas. What I hadn't told him was that even if I were well, I wouldn't have been able to go. Christmas was an incredibly hard day for me. I dreaded it every year.

Bing Crosby's soothing voice and the fat snowflakes falling peacefully outside my windows grounded me slightly. This year, tears quietly slid down my cheeks, which was better than sobbing until I had a headache, as I usually did.

Why couldn't I just remember the beautiful Christmases with my grandparents? Waking up to gifts for the first time in my life at age fifteen. My grandma's homemade biscuits and sausage gravy that she made every Christmas morning. That trip to the tree farm the day after Thanksgiving every year to choose our perfect tree and bring it home.

Those memories were a balm on the wounds from all the Christmases before. My father had died from a drug overdose on Christmas, so my grandparents easily could have chosen to feel the pain of losing their son that day rather than celebrating, but they chose to make it as joyful a day for me as they could instead.

I wanted to choose joy, but every year I ended up on my couch with a box of tissues, letting myself feel the hurt instead of burying it like I tried to do every other day of the year.

As a kid, I'd been mesmerized by holiday lights. When I saw other kids go into homes with windows trimmed with multicolored lights, I thought they must be the luckiest kids in the world. On the rare occasions I went over to another kid's house, I'd gape at their Christmas tree with homemade ornaments and shiny decorative balls, wishing my home had one, too.

It hurt to go to school after Christmas break and see the other kids wearing new clothes, talking about the games or bikes they'd been gifted. On the rare occasion someone asked me what I'd gotten for Christmas, I lied and said I got the gifts I heard everyone else saying they got.

In our house, Christmas Eve and Christmas were just regular days, when my mom was either out or in bed recovering from being out. For years, I'd been telling myself it shouldn't hurt this much. I was an adult now and I could buy myself clothes and shoes and makeup if I wanted to.

But there was something about the memory of the lovingly wrapped gifts from my grandparents, complete with glittering bows, that I couldn't replicate.

This was the last one, though. The final Christmas I'd spend all alone. Starting next year, I'd have a beautiful son or daughter to make my own memories with. I'd already started cross-stitching a stocking with an elaborate winter scene that I'd add my baby's name to when I chose one and hang up every year in our home. I'd seen stockings like this one in a magazine once as a kid and thought they were magical.

I knew now that it wasn't the stocking that was magical, but the love someone put into it just for you, adding your name and making sure you had something special. My child would feel that love every day.

After a cleansing breath, I got up from the couch and took a shower. It was late morning and I was feeling fairly human today. The gingerbread cookies were long gone, and they had tasted amazing. Since I didn't have much in the way of groceries, I went into the kitchen and started making scrambled eggs and toast.

In the living room, "Jingle Bell Rock" was playing. I was just one song from the end of the record. The thought of introducing my baby to the songs my grandparents had danced to while we decorated our tree made me smile.

How I missed them. For a long time, I'd been completely alone, and I'd told myself I was fine with it. Since becoming friends with Marlowe and Beau, though, I'd been happier. I had people who cared enough to check in when I was sick. People who wanted to spend time with me. It was nice.

I'd never envisioned getting to know Beau or meeting his family. I was grateful for the time we'd had together, though. One day, many years from now, I hoped to tell my child about the man who had given me the greatest gift of my life, and his family. No names, of course. I'd just tell my son or daughter about the bright, warm people who were all a small part of our little family of two.

As I ate, a text popped up on my phone.

Marlowe: It's too early in the day for family throw-downs about politics. I'm not even buzzed yet. How are you feeling?

Me: Better, actually. I just ate some eggs and toast and I think I'm going to binge watch Bridgerton. *Again.*

Marlowe: I'm jealous. Tell my husband Anthony I'm ready and waiting.

Me: Done. Good luck with the family.

I carried my dishes over to the sink, about to wash them when there was a knock at my door. I furrowed my brow. Marlowe or Beau?

It was doubtful it was Marlowe, because I'd just been texting with her. My heart raced as I ran my fingers through my unbrushed hair and looked down at my outfit.

I was wearing my comfiest pajama pants, which were flannel with the Grinch all over them, a worn-out University of Chicago Law School T-shirt, and a furry yellow bathrobe. *Shit.*

The knock sounded again, and I cringed. It had to be Beau, determined to drag me to Christmas dinner with his family. This was a worst-case scenario. I looked like hell, my cheeks tearstained and my hair wild. I wasn't up for seeing people today. Beau couldn't possibly understand why just walking into his parents' home with a beautiful tree and a big, loving family would likely make me burst into tears.

Steeling myself, I went to the door, unlocked it, and opened it, about to greet Beau when I stopped short. I just stared, my lips parted with shock.

It wasn't Beau standing at my door, but my mother.

I hadn't seen or heard from her in more than three years, but she looked a decade older than the last time I'd seen her. Her hair was a faded shade of dark brown with about two inches of gray roots showing, and she didn't look like she had any makeup on, which was unusual for her. By the dark circles under her eyes, I knew she hadn't slept recently.

"Hey," she said softly, smiling. "Can I come in?"

"Um, yeah." I stepped aside and she walked in.

She wore rubber slide sandals with socks. Not a great choice when it was snowing. Good choices weren't her strong suit, though.

"Hey, leave those shoes at the door and I'll go get you some slippers," I said. "Your feet have to be freezing."

She slipped out of the shoes and set them on the mat next to my door. "They are. I've been living in California, so I don't even have a coat."

One of the pockets on her oversized hoodie was hanging by a thread and the restaurant logo on the back was faded. As much as I resented my mom, it jarred me to see her this way. I imagined her drifting between widowed men with enough money to take care of her.

"Are you hungry?" I asked, handing her a pair of slippers from my hall closet.

"Yeah, I could eat," she said, taking the slippers. "Thanks."

Now that I was closer to her, I picked up on her smell. Between that and the stringy, oily look of her hair, I knew it had been a while since she last showered.

"How did you get here?" I asked her.

"Took a bus."

She was pulling off her socks, which were soaking wet. Questions I couldn't ask flew through my mind.

What the hell are you doing here? Why didn't you call first? Don't you have any other place to go? How long are you staying?

"Looks like you're having a comfy Christmas," she said, standing up. "That's the way to go. Christmas is just something stores make into a big deal so people will spend a bunch of money on stuff they don't need."

I felt that in the pit of my stomach, because she'd said it to me as a kid to explain why she didn't get me any presents. No one had the power to upset me the way my mom did, and I was already on the brink today. I had to stay focused on the things I could control and not let my emotions take over.

"I'll make you a grilled cheese and some soup," I said.

"You always did make the best grilled cheese sandwiches," she said. "Your place looks nice, Shelby."

"Thanks."

I'd learned to make a grilled cheese by the time I was five, because I knew I could stretch a loaf of bread and a package of cheese into several meals. Once I moved in with my grandparents, though, I hadn't ever eaten a grilled cheese again. It reminded me of times I wanted to forget.

Part of me hated myself for not slamming the door in her face the moment I recognized her. She'd been a terrible mother. Bipolar disorder was part of it, but she was also a selfish person who made bad choices and didn't care how they'd affected me.

"So what have you been up to?" she asked, sitting down at my kitchen table.

For the past three years? She only reached out to me when she needed something. Last time she'd been here, she wanted my help because she was being sued for unpaid rent and damages to an apartment she'd ditched. Somehow, the landlord had managed to track her down and have her served, which was an accomplishment in itself. She hadn't shown up for the hearings and he'd been granted a judgment against her. Not surprisingly, she didn't care until her tax return was garnished to pay what she owed.

"You've always been smart and you're a lawyer now," she had said. "I need you to help me get my tax refund back."

I'd told her that not only was it too late, but that I didn't practice law in New Mexico, where the judgment had been entered. She'd left pissed off and I hadn't seen her since.

With everyone else, I was a strong, direct communicator. I stated my boundaries. But with my mother, I was a kid again, silently along for the roller-coaster ride that was her life.

"Just work," I said in answer to her question. "What about you?"

"Oh, you know me. Never a dull moment."

I set the sandwich in front of her and she brushed her long bangs away from her eyes, smiling as she looked up at me. "No pickles?"

She'd always liked it when I put sandwich-sliced pickles in her grilled cheese sandwiches. I felt a flare of aggravation at our role reversal; moms were supposed to be the ones making the sandwiches.

"I don't have any," I said, turning my back and going to the sink to clean up.

"This is a great sandwich," she said, and I bristled.

I knew her. Compliments were only offered as a means of buttering me up before asking for something. Deep down, I knew it would be money. And I was ashamed of the part of me that wanted to write her a check just so she'd go away peacefully.

"Hey, can I crash here tonight?" she asked. "I'm in between places right now."

Was that the favor? I didn't like having her here, but if it was a matter of sleeping here for a night and leaving tomorrow, I'd survive.

"Sure," I said, turning to face her. "You look tired from the trip and I'm sure a shower would warm you up, so why don't you take a shower after this and you can sleep in the guest room. There are towels in the closet outside the bathroom and the guest room is the one with the bed made."

"You're pretty, you know. You could get a boyfriend if you'd clean yourself up and try."

I ignored her, leaving the kitchen and walking into the living room. I grabbed a book from my bookshelf, making sure it wasn't one about pregnancy, and sat down on the couch. The last thing I wanted was for my mom to know I was pregnant.

Though it looked like I was reading the book, I couldn't focus on anything but the fact that my mom was in my house. I was on edge, listening as she walked over to the sink and set her plate in it, then walked out to the living room.

"Guess I'll get that shower," she said. "And then I'm going to crash. I'm tired."

It was late afternoon, and I wondered how long it had been since she'd last slept. When I was a kid, she'd gone days at a time without sleep sometimes, and other times she'd slept sixteen hours a day.

I tried to pay attention to the book, which was about a WWII pilot, but I kept having to read the same sentence over and over. It wasn't until a tear splashed onto the page that I realized I was crying.

CHAPTER FOURTEEN

Beau

SHIT. Both my hands were occupied balancing the tower of dishes my mom had packaged leftovers for Shelby in, topped with a wrapped gift I didn't want to drop. How was I going to knock on her door?

I used the toe of my boot, tapping it against the door several times and hoping she'd hear it. Fortunately, she did, and she opened the door.

"Beau?"

I craned my neck to look at her around the massive stack of dishes. "Yeah, it's me. Merry Christmas."

"Merry Christmas. Come on in," she said. "What's all this?"

"My mom sent food for when you're feeling better. Everyone missed you."

I carried Shelby's loot into the kitchen and set it on her table. "You've got prime rib, ham, two kinds of potatoes, corn casserole, cranberry salad, and chocolate cheesecake."

She shook her head at the assortment of dishes and laughed. "That'll last me *days*, Beau. If I can even eat it."

Now that my view wasn't blocked by the dishes, I got my first good look at her and knew immediately that something was wrong. She wore flannel pants and a T-shirt. Her hair was wet, probably fresh from a shower, and her eyes looked red and swollen. I'd never seen her look anything but polished and put together.

"How are you feeling?" I asked her.

She sighed, her shoulders sinking. "Not as sick as yesterday, but..." She looked over her shoulder and spoke in a low tone. "I'm kind of shook up from getting an unexpected visitor."

"Oh, Jesus. Is that code for your period? Is the baby okay?"

She put a hand on her stomach, whispering now. "No, the baby's fine. It's my mom. She knocked on my door with no warning and she's asleep in my guest room right now. And I don't want her to know I'm pregnant, okay?"

"Yeah, of course."

That must have been why she'd been crying. Shelby hadn't told me much about her mom, but what I knew wasn't good. I stepped closer and wrapped my arms around her. She stiffened momentarily, but then her whole body relaxed and she sank against my chest.

"How long does she plan to be here?" I whispered near her ear.

"I don't know. She looks bad, though. I think she might be homeless."

"Damn, I'm sorry."

After a minute, she pulled away and looked up at me, tears shining in her eyes. "That was really nice of your mom to send the food. Tell her I said thanks."

The pain in her eyes tore at my heart. Shelby didn't deserve to feel this way.

"Hey," I said, cupping her cheek in my palm. "It's going to be okay."

She nodded, swiping beneath her eyes as the tears fell. "Yeah, I know. It'll be fine." She plastered on a smile. "You mentioned potatoes, and those actually sound really good. I might have some. Thanks again for dropping the food off."

"Oh, I'm not leaving," I said, taking my coat off

and hanging it on the back of a chair. "I don't know if you saw what's underneath all these containers, but I snagged my parents' Scrabble game. Thought we could play."

She smiled. "I never say no to Scrabble."

Damn, I liked seeing her smile. *Making* her smile. And I liked being close enough to smell the light, sweet fragrance of her bodywash or shampoo. Whatever it was, I liked it.

I moved the containers of food into one pile on the table, sorting out the Scrabble game and two wrapped presents.

"This one's from my parents," I said, passing her one of the presents. "And this one is from me."

She cringed. "Beau, you guys shouldn't have done that. I don't have anything for you."

I grinned. "I've got everything I need, plus a bunch of stuff in my car my family got me." I looked down at the box I'd passed her, which my mom had wrapped in paper with snowflakes all over it.

She unwrapped the present and pulled out a gray cashmere cardigan, just like the ones my mom had given my sisters and Chloe for Christmas.

"Oh my god, it's beautiful. It's so soft."

As she ran her hands over it, I saw that she was still crying. I figured I wouldn't mention it this time. She was having a hell of a time between being sick and her mom coming by, and pregnancy hormones probably weren't helping.

"Okay, open this one now," I said, passing her the small box I'd had gift wrapped in shiny silver paper with a red ribbon wrapped around it.

My heart pounded in my chest as she tore off the wrapping paper. I'd seen this in the store and known immediately that she'd love it, but still, I couldn't wait to see her reaction.

She flipped open the little blue box and looked at the necklace inside—a flat silver heart with *Mom* engraved on it. Her expression crumbled as she burst into tears.

Shit. Good or bad? Had I given her this gift at the worst possible time with her mom here?

"Sorry," she said, looking embarrassed.

"No, I'm the one who's sorry. I didn't mean to upset you."

She smiled. "No, these are happy tears. This is the most wonderful present anyone has ever given me. I love it so much, Beau. Thank you."

I grabbed the box and set it down, pulling her back into my arms. Burying her face in my chest, she cried and held on tightly. From someone who usually didn't show much emotion, her breakdown caught me by surprise.

Asher had once told me he learned the hard way

that women didn't want to be grilled when they were crying; they wanted to be comforted. So I just held Shelby, wishing I had the words to make her feel better but knowing I probably didn't.

"Sorry," she said, pulling away after a minute and avoiding my gaze. "Christmas is always a hard day for me. I should have mentioned that."

She walked over to the kitchen sink and took a paper towel from the holder on the counter, wiping her cheeks.

"Want to talk about it?" I asked.

She exhaled heavily as she threw away the paper towel. "My dad died on Christmas. It was a really long time ago, but still."

"I'm so sorry."

"It's not just that. The only people who have ever given me Christmas gifts—other than you, just now—are my grandparents, after I moved in with them. Unless the bonus from the firm I worked for after law school counts. But like, a real present with paper and a bow…just them, and now you. And your parents."

Jesus. I'd had it so good my whole life. Shelby hadn't moved in with her grandparents until she was fifteen. It killed me to picture her as a little girl, losing her dad on Christmas and never getting a single gift.

"I'm going to heat up some potatoes," she said, walking over to the table to look through the containers I'd brought over. "Do you want anything?"

"No, thanks. I'm still stuffed from earlier."

While she put mashed potatoes and gravy into a bowl and microwaved it, I opened the box with the necklace I'd bought her and took it out, then walked over to her.

"Can I put it on you?" I asked.

She smiled, nodded, and turned around, gathering her hair and picking it up to expose her neck.

I was close enough to smell her shampoo again. I looped the necklace around her neck and tried to fasten the clasp at the back.

"This thing is made for much smaller hands than mine," I muttered. "Hang on."

After several tries, I got the damn thing clasped, pretty much on accident since I could hardly see it. She turned around and met my eyes, touching the heart with her fingertips.

"I'll never take it off," she said. "And when I look at it, I'll always think of everything you've done for me."

Her eyes glistened again, and I felt a powerful pull to show her just how amazing she was. How could I be the only one besides her grandparents to see it? The world had beaten her down, time and again, and she'd gotten up each time despite all of it. Chasing your dreams took guts, and Shelby had more guts than anyone I'd ever known.

I didn't even bother telling myself it was a bad idea. Fuck it. I cupped her cheek and leaned close, my lips hovering an inch from hers for a couple of seconds so she had time to tell me to stop if she wanted to.

She didn't, though. When our lips met, a jolt ran from the tip of my spine to the base. Her mouth was soft and she kissed me back tentatively, but it wasn't enough. I'd wanted this for so damn long now that I couldn't hold back.

I slid my hand around to the back of her neck, my other hand finding her hip and then the small of her back. Did I pull her closer or did she move closer? All I knew for sure was that our bodies had molded to each other at some point, her soft curves pressing against me in all the right places.

When our tongues met for the first time and I felt her moan softly into my mouth, I pulled her more firmly against my hips so she could feel how hard I was for her. Christ, I wanted her bad.

Her hand combed through my hair, tugging on it. I groaned and lifted her onto the kitchen counter, never breaking the kiss.

She pulled her mouth from mine suddenly, her cheeks flushed and her breathing hard.

"Is this a pity thing?" she asked.

What the fuck? Did she think I could choose to set myself on fire for her because she was having a rough day?

"Does it feel like a pity thing?" I asked gruffly.

"No."

I held her gaze, lifting the bottom of her shirt up a few inches to expose her stomach. She squirmed in response.

"Can I stand for this?" she asked softly. "I have rolls when I'm sitting."

I shook my head. "I love your body. I fantasize about it constantly."

Her eyes widened. "You do?"

I stepped back and unbuttoned my flannel shirt, watching the rise and fall of her chest as she watched me. I went slowly, unfastening one button at a time. When I finished, I dropped the shirt to the ground and her gaze wandered over my chest, shoulders, and arms.

"I didn't think you'd have a hairy chest," she said softly, running her fingertips over it. "But I like it."

I burned for her in a way I'd never known. Her touch sent a current through my body, making me want to bury myself inside her.

"Let me see you," I said, reaching for her shirt again.

She slid down from the counter and pulled her shirt up and over her head, her expression vulnerable when her eyes found mine again. My erection pressed uncomfortably against the fly of my jeans as I took her in, her breasts cupped by a simple cream-colored satin bra.

"You're so beautiful," I said softly. "Even more beautiful than I could have ever imagined."

Something flared in her eyes, a mixture of confidence and arousal. When I put my hands on her hips, on the edge of devouring her, she stopped me with a palm to my chest.

"Can we go to my bedroom?" she asked.

Hell yes we could. I took her hand and she led the way through the living room, down a short hallway, and then through the doorway of a darkened room, closing it behind us.

"I didn't think I could feel good today," she said, her voice so low it was almost inaudible. "You take away my sadness, though."

Her warm breath danced against my chin and I took her in my arms, kissing her with all the pent-up desire I'd felt since that day at the doctor's office. It was finally happening. My fantasies about being her first were coming true.

She unbuttoned my pants and pushed them down, and I did the same to hers. Then I walked her over to the bed.

"Get on your knees on the bed," I whispered in her ear. "Don't bend down, just get on your knees and face away from me."

She did, and I could just make out her outline in the dim light of the room. God, she was gorgeous. Her breasts were big, probably *D* cups, and her ass was round and sexy. There wasn't an inch of her I didn't want to touch and taste.

I wrapped my arms around her from behind and kissed her neck, my erection pressing against her back. When I cupped her breasts, she moaned and arched back against me.

She was so fucking responsive. I was on the edge of losing my already limited self-control. When I slid my hand down her stomach and cupped her pussy through her panties, she inhaled sharply. It was all I could do not to push her panties down and fuck her from behind.

Not yet anyway. I slid the straps of her bra down to her shoulders and pushed the cups down, exposing her nipples. When I ran my fingertips around one of them, her moan was long and desperate.

I unfastened her bra and teased her nipples and

breasts until she was panting, then slid my hand inside her panties and slowly slid a finger inside her. She squirmed, her body begging me to go further. I moved my hand back out, though, hungry for more of her desperation for me.

She turned then, taking my hand and pulling me toward the bed as she lay down on her back. This was fucking dangerous. I wanted to be inside her virgin pussy so bad my hands were shaking.

I kissed her and she ran her hands through my hair again, pulling on it as she gently bit my lip. I'd expected her to be tentative in bed, unsure of herself, but I was wrong. Shelby had always told me exactly what she'd wanted—it was one of my favorite things about her.

"At least you can't get me pregnant," she said in a teasing tone.

She reached between us and ran her hand over my erection, letting out a surprised moan. I closed my eyes, forcing myself to hold on. To keep some shred of control.

"I want you, Beau," she said softly. "Make love to me, just this one time."

Just one time. You take away my sadness.

Fuck. I moved away from her.

"Not like this," I said. "I'm sorry. I want you more than you can possibly imagine, but not like this."

"Not like what?" She grabbed at the bedcovers, pulling them over herself even though I could hardly see her.

"When you're upset and want me to make your pain go away. With your mom in the next room. Telling me it's only going to be this one time."

One time? Fuck that. If that was all she was willing to give me, I wasn't taking it.

"You should go," she said, her tone angry and hurt.

"I don't want to go," I said. "Can we just start this night over? I came here to spend the evening with you."

"We can't just get dressed and act like all that didn't happen." She was on the verge of tears again, but this time, it was my fault. "Just go. Please."

Great. I'd made her shitty Christmas even worse. I picked up my jeans and put them on, then walked into the kitchen to find my shirt.

She didn't even leave the bedroom, so once I was dressed, I grabbed my coat and left, wishing I'd done things a whole lot differently.

CHAPTER FIFTEEN

Shelby

"HEY, I need your opinion on my outfit," Marlowe said when I opened my apartment door.

"Sure, come on in."

I kept the disappointment from my tone. It wasn't that I was bummed Marlowe was here, but that my heart had been pounding when I heard the knock in hopes it was Beau.

It was New Year's Eve—six days since he'd left my apartment. He'd texted the next day apologizing, which made it even worse. It hurt knowing he was sorry for something that had made me feel more alive than I had in years.

"Hi Tracy," Marlowe said when she saw my mom

sitting on the couch.

She'd stayed Christmas night and never said anything about leaving. And she'd been grilling me about who had come over on Christmas because I'd left the empty box from the gift Beau had given me on the kitchen table and she'd seen it before I got up the next day.

Rookie mistake. She was like a dog with a bone now, refusing to let go because she knew from that little blue box that I'd been given an expensive gift by a man. I faithfully kept the necklace tucked inside my shirt collar so she wouldn't see it, but she knew something was up.

"Marlowe, you look like a little firecracker," my mom said, smiling.

Marlowe's eyes widened with alarm, probably because who wanted to look like a firecracker? She wore a strapless, super short, sparkly gold dress with fringe on the bottom, and she had a thin, glittery gold headband tucked into her short hair.

"You look amazing," I said. "Remember it's New Year's Eve so you need to have that extra punch."

"Yeah?" She smiled, looking hopeful. "It's the shoes that are giving me fits. None of my gold shoes look right with this dress, so I'm stuck with these."

She wore black heels with thin straps that laced halfway up her calf.

"I think they look great," I said.

"They're starting to grow on me."

"So you're going out with the accountant again?"

She grinned. "Theo. He's basically a younger Idris Elba if Idris was an eight instead of a ten. Like, tall, broad shoulders and very handsome, but not *can't look away, my ovaries just incinerated*, you know?"

"Ovaries are important. I recommend keeping them intact."

"Where's he taking you for dinner?" my mom asked.

Marlowe glanced at her, then back at me. I'd texted her the day after Christmas about my mom showing up and told her about what went down with Beau. It was pretty much a novel broken up into dozens of texts. Marlowe didn't think my mom should have dropped in unannounced, didn't think she should be staying without being invited, and was ready and willing to kick her out if I said the word.

"We're going to a party his boss is hosting," Marlowe said to me in indirect answer to my mom's question.

"Ew, no," my mom said. "He's not even paying for a nice dinner? Any guy who expects you to get by on celery sticks and free drinks isn't worth it."

Marlowe glared at me, silently asking for permission to tell my mom to go to hell. I mouthed *I'm sorry*, wishing for the thousandth time that I had a mother who didn't embarrass me.

It was her mental illness. That was the thing that kept me hanging on, unable to cut her out of my life for good. Ironically, her bipolar disorder was hard to treat because of her bipolar disorder. She went through ups and downs, often thinking during her ups that she didn't need her medication anymore.

"I better go. He's picking me up soon," Marlowe said, reaching for my hand and squeezing it. "Happy New Year, Shelby. Becoming friends with you was one of the best things that happened to me this year. We're going to slay this new year together."

I squeezed her hand in return, grateful she'd stopped by. It was a reminder that I wasn't alone anymore. Marlowe knew I didn't want my mom to know I was pregnant, so she kept that on the down-low, but I could feel the encouragement in her gaze.

This time next year, I'd have a baby to ring in the new year with. I pictured us in silly hats, probably sacked out before the ball dropped. It sounded perfect to me.

"We should order some food," my mom said after Marlowe left. "How does Chinese sound?"

It sounded terrible. I wasn't throwing up from pregnancy sickness anymore, but I still felt queasy and exhausted most of the time and trying to hide it from my mom wasn't easy. Since I didn't have much energy for cooking, we'd been having food delivered every day.

Whether it sounded good or not, though, my growing baby needed nourishment.

"I'll call in an order," I said. "What do you want?"

"Chicken fried rice and egg rolls. You should sit down and rest after that. You look tired. I'm going to clean the bathroom."

I pressed my lips together to hold in my sharp comment. I'd never known my mom to volunteer to clean a bathroom or wash dishes, but she'd washed the dishes a couple of times since being here. Not that there were many, but still. Maybe she was finally getting her life together.

"We should go get our hair done next week," I said. "And pedicures, too. My treat."

Everything was my treat, because I was pretty sure she was penniless. But the money didn't matter. I'd never done things with my mom that other mothers and daughters did, and if she was willing to try, I was, too.

"That sounds really nice," she said, getting up from the couch. "Where can I find cleaning supplies?"

"In the cabinet under the sink."

I ordered our food, surprised my mom was still

cleaning the bathroom when it arrived forty-five minutes later. After we ate, she went back to work and I curled up on the couch, scrolling on my phone and wishing Beau would text.

Things would never be the same between us. Our easy friendship was gone now, replaced by the awkwardness of…whatever that night was. Had we almost slept together? I'd been ready to, and that was a big deal for me. Years ago, there had been one other man I'd wanted that with, but we broke up before the time was right.

For a few incredible minutes on Christmas, I'd felt beautiful to Beau. Desirable. Like half of a whole. Not like we were going to be a couple afterward or anything, but like I was exactly what he wanted and needed for that one night, as he was for me.

The worst part was, I hadn't thought of him that way until he gave me the necklace. I was deliberately trying to keep him at arm's length since I didn't want him to have regrets about agreeing to not have any relationship with my child when it was born.

Being friendly was nice, because it would help me tell my son or daughter what kind of man their father was one day.

When he'd walked into my apartment with leftovers and that gift, though…I'd let my guard down. All the way down. I'd imagined what it would be like to be with Beau, and then he'd kissed me and it wasn't so imaginary anymore.

I knew what it felt like to be touched and kissed by him, held and cared for by him. I'd given up on hoping for those things, and he'd brought back the hope and then pulled the rug out from under me.

Damn him. I vowed to start the new year looking forward instead of backward. Between work, pregnancy, and my mom, I had enough on my plate already.

I woke up in the evening after falling asleep on the couch and saw my mom asleep in a nearby recliner. The TV was on, and when I focused on the screen, Beau was there, playing a game at the Shapiro Center, the Coyotes' home ice.

Though I should have grabbed the remote and turned the channel, I couldn't. The game was tied 1–1, and I felt a small thrill every time Beau had control of the puck. He moved up and down the ice as easily as if he were running, executing plays with his teammates without even needing to look at them.

"Beau Fox is on a hot streak," one of the announcers said. "He's scored at least one goal in the past three games. Let's see if he keeps that streak going tonight."

"He and Harrison and Grazer play in lockstep,"

the other announcer said. "If the Coyotes' defense shows up to a game, that first line is pretty much unstoppable."

During a timeout, the cameras showed the cheering crowd, which included Beau's fan club, the Foxes. It blew my mind that those women showed up to every home game to hold up signs saying, "Fox rocks my socks." One of them wore a T-shirt with a picture of his smiling face on it.

Reality hit me hard and fast. I was a fool, catching feelings for a man who was a literal superstar. Beau had been right to stop things that night. I'd be better off dying a virgin than giving myself away to a man with triple-digit notches on his bedpost.

My mom woke up, her face scrunched in confusion. "How long was I out?"

"I don't know. It's almost seven."

"Wow." She got up from the chair and picked up the remote. "You're not watching this, are you?"

"No."

Tie game or not, I couldn't fixate on anything involving Beau. It could only end one way—with my heart broken.

I was fortunate to have a part of him in my child. That would have to be enough.

"Should we watch the ball drop?" my mom asked.

"Sure."

It was the first New Year's Eve in years I wasn't alone. A year ago, I wouldn't have dreamed I'd spend it with my mom, expecting a baby of my own.

My life was quiet and simple, but I liked it that way. It was enough.

———

THE NEXT MORNING, I woke up more rested than I had in a long time. I didn't feel the need to reach for the saltine crackers on my nightstand to settle my stomach.

I hoped pregnancy sickness was one of several things I could leave behind for good on the first day of the new year. Mom and I could go get groceries and maybe go out for a movie or do some shopping. Maybe it was time to tell her I was pregnant.

I got up and peeked in the doorway of the guest room, but it was empty, the covers a tangled mess.

"Mom?" I called out, walking into the kitchen.

It was empty, too. Maybe she was running an errand. I started some water in my teapot and went to the living room to look out the big picture window and see how much snow we'd gotten the night before.

My gaze stopped on my desk as I walked past my office nook. My laptop was gone. I always kept it in the same place, on the left-hand side of my desk, and there was a bare spot where it usually was.

My heart thundered with worry. I had confidential work for clients on that laptop, and even though it was encrypted, nothing was unbreakable.

And worse than that was knowing deep down what had happened to it. Why did I trust anyone but myself? I never seemed to learn.

I ran to my bedroom in a panic, praying I'd find my most treasured possession—the silver Tiffany watch my grandma had left me. My grandpa had given it to her for their fiftieth wedding anniversary and unlike the computer, it was irreplaceable. He'd had it engraved on the back with *I love you, Sunshine,* his nickname for her.

My jewelry box was on a shelf in my walk-in closet, and tears filled my eyes when I saw that one of the drawers wasn't all the way closed. Someone other than me had gotten into it.

A couple of rings that weren't worth much were gone, and so was the watch. I sat down on the edge of my bed and sobbed into my hands.

I'd been burned hard twice in the span of a week. And this time I'd let my mom do it to me, trusting her when she'd proven to me so many times that I shouldn't.

Never again.

CHAPTER SIXTEEN

Beau

Three months later

"Check it out." Our backup goalie, Drew Horner, turned the screen of his cell phone around so I could see it. "That's my niece, Shelby Grace McNeil."

"She's a cutie," I said, smiling at the picture of a red-faced newborn wearing a bow the size of her entire face.

"Yep, I'm an uncle now. I can't wait to buy Shelby her first hockey stick."

I nodded, my mind a million miles away.

Shelby. Hearing her name reminded me of the woman I'd been trying my best to forget about for three months now. I'd texted and called several times after Christmas, but she'd made it clear she wanted nothing to do with me.

I was at war with myself for the first month, torn between wanting to respect her wishes and knowing she was wrong. There was something between us, and it had caught me entirely by surprise that night. I knew I was intrigued by her and I felt an attraction, but I'd been able to stop myself from acting on it before then because I knew it wasn't a good idea.

Seeing her vulnerable side had changed everything, though. When she'd opened herself up to me like she did on Christmas, I couldn't have stopped myself from kissing her if I'd wanted to. And I didn't.

I was pulled to her in a way so magnetic I was powerless to stop it. When we'd kissed, it lit me up from the inside out. I'd never felt anything like it. Stopping things with her that night was one of the hardest things I'd ever done.

She didn't believe me when I'd said I wanted her, but not like that. Not when she just wanted me to make the pain go away. Her wounded pride told her lies, and she wouldn't listen to the truth.

I got it. She'd been hurt and lied to a lot in life. Not by me, though. I was being punished for other people's mistakes.

"You planning on playing tonight?" Dalton

asked me.

"Huh?" I looked up at him from the locker room bench, where I'd been lost in thought. "Yeah, just thinking about something."

"Something or someone?"

I shrugged. "Both, I guess."

"Check out my niece," Horner said to Dalton, showing him the same photo he'd shown me.

"She looks like you," Dalton said.

"You think?"

"Yeah, you make that same face when you get pissed about something."

Horner gave him the finger and moved on to show his niece's photo to someone else. Dalton seemed to sense that I wasn't in a mood to talk, and he moved on, too.

I didn't just think of Shelby often, but also the baby she was carrying. It was the size of a big leek now, according to the weekly notifications I got. He or she could smile.

Was Shelby still getting sick all the time? Had her mom ever left? I had lots of questions, but no answers. My family had stopped asking about her a while ago, probably assuming we'd been a thing and weren't anymore.

It fucking grated on me, the way things had gone down between us. Shelby hadn't given us a fair chance. I knew it was a bad idea for us to get involved, but something had clicked into place that night and I couldn't undo it. She was on my mind all the time, still the object of every sexual fantasy I had. And she wanted nothing to do with me.

"Gentlemen," Mila said, storming into the locker room like she owned the place.

Which, she kind of did. The team at least. And when she had something to say, she didn't ask Coach when would be a good time. She just showed up and said what was on her mind.

This time, she stood near the center of the locker room, just to the side of the team logo on the carpet that she knew better than to step on. Everyone quieted to listen.

"We have a twenty-three-man roster," she said, looking from face to face. "That's forty-six balls, if my math is correct. And yet..." She raised her voice. "I'm not seeing any balls out on the ice, guys. Where are the balls? The guts? The heart?"

We'd dropped our last two games, both on the road, and I couldn't deny she was right. We'd played like a team phoning it in, me included. If we wanted to make the playoffs, we were going to have to turn things around fast.

"I care whether we win or lose," she said sharply. "Does anyone else?"

Coach stood to the side, his arms crossed and his expression grim. None of us liked Mila in here busting our balls, even if she was right. It wasn't her job.

"Show me something out there tonight, guys," she said. "I don't even care what it is, just *something*. Something that makes the game feel more hockey and less like a piano recital. This is your home ice. Give our fans something to get excited about. Balls out, for fuck's sake."

No one responded, but she never waited for a response. As soon as the last word was out of her mouth, she stormed back out of the locker room, her gaze on the door until she was gone.

"She's a sweetheart," Colby muttered from nearby.

It was almost time to leave the locker room for the game. Though it had been almost three months since Shelby and I had talked, something made me grab my phone from my locker and send her a text.

Me: I'm thinking about you. I miss you.

I had more to say, but for now, that would have to do. If she didn't respond, I'd stop by her apartment. I knew in my gut that things weren't over between us.

She might never give me another shot, but I wasn't giving up without a fight.

CHAPTER SEVENTEEN

Shelby

"So there I am, finally about to get the *D*, when that motherfucker says 'Guide me in, baby,'" Marlowe's podcast guest said. "Like what the hell, bro? You've got one job here. I'm not grabbing your dick and sticking it in for you."

Marlowe hummed in sympathy. "Buzzkill. I was once with a guy who could *not* get it in. Not to save his life. He tried and tried while I lay there staring at the ceiling. He eventually deflated and wanted me to suck it."

"Glen," Marlowe said from my couch, where she was lying while we listened to her most recent podcast. "Never date a guy named Glen." She looked over to make sure I was paying attention. "Listen to this part; it's my worst sexual encounter ever."

"…waited like several months to have sex because I really liked him," podcast Marlowe said. "He was funny and cute and we had the best conversations. But then when we finally had sex, oh my god, girl."

Her guest laughed. "Been there, my friend."

"With every thrust, he made this noise, like *uhh*, and that was bad enough, but then he started talking, and it was like How Not to Dirty Talk 101. He was like, 'You feel that? You feel my penis in your vagina?'"

I laughed along with Marlowe's guest, whose voice was coming from the speaker on Marlowe's phone.

"No, that's not even the worst part," podcast Marlowe said. "I was trying to disassociate myself from what he was saying so I'd have a chance of at least getting an orgasm out of all this, but then he starts saying 'I can feel your uterus. You like the way my penis pokes your uterus?'"

Her guest howled with laughter. "He did not!"

"He did!" Marlowe said, turning from her position on my couch to face me. "That happened. Every single word was true. I seriously thought I might be on some hidden camera show where he was trying to make it the most terrible, comical sex imaginable, but sadly, it was real."

"Did you stop seeing him after that?" I asked.

"He was so great in every other area that I tried to train him. I told him silence was my kink, but he said he couldn't get into it without making it a whole production, so…I broke it off."

I thought about Christmas night with Beau. The things he said to me made my entire body hum with arousal. It was the first time I'd kissed a man and felt no awkwardness. With Beau, I just knew what to say and do.

Pregnancy hormones had shifted from making me sick in the first trimester to making me horny in the second, so my vibrator had gotten a workout. Every time, I fantasized that Beau hadn't stopped that night, or that he showed up on my doorstep saying he'd been wrong and he wanted me immediately.

It was ironic, fantasizing about being with the man who had said he wanted to be with me when I'd told him to stay away. But fantasies always had a happy ending; reality didn't.

"Read me the text again," Marlowe said.

I didn't even have to look at my phone to recite it; I'd read it at least fifty times already. "I'm thinking about you. I miss you."

We were having a lazy Sunday afternoon. After going out for lunch, Marlowe and I had come back to my apartment and started listening to some of Marlowe's recorded podcasts. Marlowe was on the couch and I was kicked back in my favorite recliner. She'd turned off the podcast, but I'd be finishing it on my own later.

I was proud of her. She'd recently gotten a big advertiser for the podcast because her subscription numbers were growing rapidly. She had a way of making listeners feel like they were chatting with a close girlfriend.

"And he sent it last night?" she asked.

"Yeah, early evening."

"I don't know how you kept yourself from responding, girl. Or why. He's hot, successful, and sweet, and you're pregnant with his kid. What more do you want?"

I smiled, because we'd had this conversation over and over in the three months since I'd stopped speaking to Beau.

"I just feel like I'm better off alone," I said. "It's not because there's anything wrong with him. My plan was to have this baby on my own, and I'm sticking to the plan."

"No, you got offended when he didn't want to have sex with you. Or I guess he wanted to but didn't want your first time to be with your mom in the next room. Which I get. And then your mom screwed you over the next day and you wrote both of them off for it. You were wrong."

I'd had plenty of time to reflect on things, and I knew she was right. I'd overreacted. But I'd also thought a lot about how dangerous it was to get involved with Beau, because if he developed a relationship with our baby and things didn't work out between us, he could sue me for visitation.

That was what really burned, and I was ashamed of the reasons for it. When I thought about our child spending time at Henry and Claire Fox's home, surrounded by warmth and love and luxury, or going to the hockey games of their superstar father, and then returning to me, I felt inadequate.

I'd never admit it out loud to anyone, but deep down, I feared that Beau would marry a beautiful, outgoing woman who was everything I wasn't and our child would prefer being with him and his family to being with me, a loner introvert.

I hated that feeling not good enough was so ingrained into who I was, but my fears and worries came from years of being looked past, ignored, and neglected. While I could put on a brave, confident face, deep down I felt inadequate.

"Text him back, Shelby," Marlowe implored. "Tell

him the truth, whatever it is. I know you miss him, don't even bother denying it."

"I do miss him," I admitted.

She moved into a sitting position, her eyes sparkling. "Text him back right now. Be brave. I know you have it in you to tell him something real."

"I'm always real," I countered defensively.

"No, you're not. Not when it comes to him. If you ignore him, that's a response. It says you don't care enough to respond. And you do care. I see it all over your face right now."

I rubbed my hand over my baby bump, not bothering with a passive aggressive response. We both knew she was right.

"Okay," I said, trying to sound nonchalant. "I'll respond."

"All I ask is that you respond bravely," she said. "Vulnerability is brave."

"Are you starting a new podcast where you psychoanalyze people?"

She laughed. "Better than psychoanalyzing myself. I'm a hot mess, but at least I can admit it."

I glared at her as I picked up my phone. Marlowe was younger than me, but she was wiser.

Things had gotten messy between me and Beau. We'd gone off script, and I didn't want things between us to end with his awkward Christmas departure from my apartment. If nothing else, we needed to clear the air.

"Ask him a question," Marlowe said. "That's how you tell him you want him to text back."

My fingers were poised to type out a text when I paused. Did I really want to open myself up to Beau again? I'd spent New Year's Day calling pawnshops in the area to see if I could track down my laptop and my grandma's watch—and I'd succeeded. I'd given myself that one day to feel sorry for myself over both Beau and my mom, and then I'd closed the door behind me and moved forward.

I still saw his smile in my mind, though. Every day. And the little crinkles that appeared by his eyes when he smiled. I heard his hearty laugh and relived the feel of his skilled hands on my body. No matter how hard I tried, I couldn't forget.

Me: I miss you too. How have you been?

My heart raced as I stared at my phone screen, waiting and hoping for those three little dots indicating that he was texting me back. After about thirty seconds, they did.

Beau: I've been busy with hockey. Can I see you? Soon?

"He wants to see me," I told Marlowe.

She grinned. "You have to say yes. I think he's the real deal, Shelby."

He was the real deal for now, but how long would that last? Beau had agreed to be my sperm donor, but what would happen between us once the baby was born?

All the unknowns made my pulse pound with worry.

"Look, even if you guys are never anything but good friends, don't you at least want that?" Marlowe asked.

"Enough already. I'm going to see him," I said, giving her a wide-eyed look of annoyance.

"Now?"

I laughed. "Will you stop?"

With a deep breath, I texted Beau back.

Me: How about dinner this week?

Beau: Sounds great. I'm free on Wednesday and Thursday.

Me: I have my prenatal yoga class on Wednesday, so Thursday would be good.

Beau: Pick you up at 6?

I hesitated, because I'd suggested dinner so we could meet on neutral ground. If we stood in my apartment and he gave me that look again, like he did right before he kissed me on Christmas, I'd melt into a puddle at his feet.

He'd picked me up for dinner before, though. I'd handled it then.

That was prekiss, Shelby, my inner voice said in warning. *Before you knew what his erection felt like pressed against you.*

It was dinner. Nothing more. I texted him back.

Me: See you then.

"He's picking me up Thursday at six for dinner," I told Marlowe, setting my phone down, leaning back and putting both hands on my pregnant belly.

"Can I hide inside your apartment so I can spy when he picks you up? It'll be easier for us to break it down after if I can see it and hear it."

"No," I said, laughing, not even considering it.

She grunted in disapproval. "Fine. And just FYI, it's perfectly safe to have sex when you're pregnant. Just don't let him put all his weight on the baby and squish it."

I gaped at her. "We're going to dinner, not having sex."

"He might want to eat more than dinner, girl."

I laughed, because my outraged comments only fueled her to push my buttons even more. Marlowe had brought much needed levity into my life.

"You could be a little coy," she suggested. "Don't give him the *P.* Maybe just some oral or anal."

I busted out laughing at that. "Oral and anal is coy now? Good to know."

"When you're a virgin, it is."

"I feel weird about oral and downright indignant about anal," I said. "I don't think I'd enjoy either."

"Oh, oral is spectacular, as long as you're with a guy who knows what he's doing. Have I ever told you about the guy who tried to get me off by licking the wrong end of my hoo-hah? The end by my butt-hole. I gently moved his head and positioned his head over my clit—this was a grown man, by the way; we weren't teenagers—and he goes 'what are you doing' and I'm like, 'that's my clit,' and he goes, 'No it's not.' He was all condescending, like I didn't know where my own fucking clitoris was. He said it was inside me and he knew just the spot."

"Have you *ever* had good sex?" I asked her, shaking my head.

"Yes, but the bad is more memorable. I'm pretty sure Beau will know what he's doing."

"Well, it doesn't matter because it's just dinner."

"Keep telling yourself that, sweetie. But you still need to go to a salon and get your lady junk groomed, because I'm guessing you're past being able to reach it by now."

CHAPTER EIGHTEEN

Shelby

"Hey," Beau said, smiling at me when I opened my door. "You look great."

My hair was a little longer and my belly was a lot bigger than when he'd seen me last. He was clean-shaven, wearing a polo shirt and jeans. As always, it was his eyes that drew me in. My heart raced as I fought the desire to throw myself at him.

"Thanks," I said. "You do too."

His gaze landed on my bump, which was looking more like a mountain every day. "How's the baby?"

"Everything's good. I didn't find out the sex, but I'm dying to know. It's a healthy baby so far, though, so that's the most important thing."

"Good." His eyes radiated warmth when they met mine again. "Ready to go?"

I nodded, even though emotionally I was all over the map. I'd planned to be friendly, but not let him affect me. I wanted us to set things right between us, but I didn't want my body to be throwing an inner parade upon seeing him again. It was, though. I wanted to be over it in terms of our attraction, but clearly, I wasn't.

I grabbed my bag and locked up, and we walked out to his car together.

"Your arms look bigger," I said.

"Yeah?" He grinned at me and flexed. "My trainer has had me working more on arms."

"Hey, guys!" Marlowe approached us, feigning surprise. "You must be Beau. I'm Shelby's friend Marlowe."

She was terrible at this. I wished I would have just let her hide in my apartment since we left a few seconds after Beau arrived.

"Marlowe, I've heard a lot about you," he said as she went in for a quick hug.

"Same. It's good to finally meet you."

"We're going out for dinner," I said. "Where are you off to?"

"Oh, Target run," she said, waving a hand. "Need me to pick anything up for you?"

"I think I'm good."

"Spicy Doritos?"

I hesitated. I'd had some Doritos over at Marlowe's a couple of months ago and now I was addicted. Since they weren't good for the baby, I didn't buy them for myself, but she kept a steady supply in her apartment for me. I called her my Doritos dealer.

"No, that's okay," I said.

"I'll get some for my place," she said, winking.

"Hey, I'll take some, too," Beau said with a grin. "I love Doritos."

"We have to go," I said. "I'll talk to you tomorrow, Marlowe."

"Text me anytime."

I cringed inwardly. Though I loved her, I didn't want Beau to know my best friend was waiting with bated breath for updates about our evening. It was just dinner.

Beau opened the passenger side door for me like no time had passed. I paused as I was about to get inside, too swayed by the intensity of his blue-eyed gaze to look away.

He wrapped his arms around me and pulled me close into a hug. I went stiff for one surprised second, but then I relaxed against him.

"I really missed you," he said, his warm breath dancing on my skin.

"Me too."

He pulled back and looked into my eyes, a small smile playing on his lips. "I've got things I want to say to you, but not in a parking lot. I'll wait until we get to the restaurant."

I nodded and stepped into the car, my mouth suddenly dry. Even though I was wearing black maternity pants with an elastic waistband and a top that tied beneath my breasts and had flowy fabric billowing over my very pregnant stomach, Beau still looked at me the same way he had on Christmas. There was still affection and I was pretty sure...desire.

I'd never felt less attractive, but when he looked at me just now, something shifted inside me. I felt like a woman again, with needs and wants and feelings, instead of a baby-growing vessel.

"How's your knee?" I asked him once he was inside the car, hoping to steer the conversation to a place that would allow my heart to settle into its usual rhythm.

I'd kept up with watching hockey games when I could during the past three months, and I'd followed hockey news online, too. Not exactly the behavior of a woman who was over it.

Beau had sprained his knee about six weeks ago, missing two weeks' worth of games while he healed.

"It's a lot better," he said. "I was lucky, it was just a mild sprain. The team trainer has had me doing a lot of physical therapy."

"It's healed up okay, though?"

"Yep. Good as new. But the doctor said I'm probably going to be prone to arthritis as I age."

"My grandpa had arthritis. He always said his joints should be on the payroll at the local TV station because they were better at knowing when it was going to rain or snow than the weather forecasters were."

Beau grinned over at me. "Something to look forward to, I guess."

"How's your family?"

"Everybody's good. Mom and Dad are doing their thing as always, same with Asher and Chloe and the kids, and Fiona will be having her baby any day now. It's a girl."

"Aw, good for her." I put my hand on my bump, eager for the day when I was close to delivering.

"Isaac and I put together her nursery furniture a couple of weeks ago because Adrian is a douchebag who said he didn't have time to do it."

"Yikes, and this is the guy she's going to be relying on for help with their baby?"

Beau shrugged. "Adrian can't be relied on for anything unless it's something he wants to do. Asher, Isaac, me, and Genevieve have all told Fiona about how we feel about him, but our parents aren't so blunt."

"That's a shame. Fiona deserves better."

Beau exhaled hard and glanced over at me. "Yeah, I can't wait until we get to the restaurant. I've already waited three months to say this stuff to you. I'm sorry for every stupid thing I said or did that drove you away. That was the last thing I wanted."

"I know, and…me too. I'm sorry for the way things went down."

"You just cut me off," he said, looking straight ahead as he drove. "You wouldn't even respond to my texts. I was worried about you."

"It wasn't just about you. Something else happened, too, and I just needed to retreat for a little while. Be alone with myself."

He pulled the car into a random parking lot and then angled the car into a parking spot before turning to look over at me. "What else happened?"

I didn't want to say the words out loud. I'd told Marlowe about it over text, and that had been hard enough. Beau had amazing parents; I was ashamed of mine. He already knew about my mom, though, and I hadn't lied to him before. I didn't want to start now.

"When I woke up New Year's Day, my mom was gone, and she took my laptop and the Tiffany watch my grandma left me."

"Holy shit, she stole from you?"

I felt a flare of aggravation, because *yes, obviously*. His shock only made what was already bad feel even worse.

"Yes. I told you, she's bipolar."

"That doesn't mean she's incapable of knowing right from wrong."

I closed my eyes, trying not to lash out at him. "Well, I've known her my whole life and you've never met her. She's used people for money her entire life. Usually men, but now that she's not as young and attractive as she once was, I imagine that's harder."

He reached over and took my hand.

"You deserve better. You know that, right?"

I laughed bitterly. "Since when do any of us get what we deserve? I got the mother I got."

"Look, the last thing I want is to piss you off again, but you need to know you shouldn't just shrug this off because it's the way she's always been. Don't let her in your apartment ever again."

My throat tightened. "I don't want to, but on

Christmas, she walked to my house from the bus station in a pair of rubber sandals in the snow. No coat. She was hungry and freezing. And I may seem cold and analytical, but she is *my mother*. I don't think she had anywhere else to go."

"Hey," he said softly, cupping my cheek and turning my face so our gazes met. "You don't seem cold and analytical. You're warm and sweet. You're amazing. I don't want you to resign yourself to being hurt again and again."

Tears slipped from the corners of my eyes onto my cheeks. "That's been my life so far."

"Shelby, you twisted what I said that night to make it fit your narrative. I wanted you so goddamn much, and I still do, but you're special and I wanted you to know that." He gave me an imploring look. "I won't let you down. I'm not looking for a quick lay. I knew all along that it would be safer if we kept things platonic, but I couldn't deny what I felt for you anymore on Christmas. It's too strong. I can't even explain it."

A man pounded on the car window on my side, making me jump with alarm. Beau scowled and opened his door, getting out to talk to the man.

"What the fuck, man? She's pregnant."

The man pointed at a sign on the side of the building next to the lot we were parked in. "This lot is for paying customers only. Get inside the store or get going."

"Yeah, we're leaving, asshole."

He got back in the car, started it and backed out. I took a few breaths in and out, my emotions running wild from our conversation.

"So anyway," Beau said. "Are you seeing anyone?"

I gaped at him. "What? No."

"Good, because that guy would have been regretting that choice about this time tomorrow. Give me another chance."

"Another chance? You mean…sex?"

"I mean all of it. Give me a chance to be the man in your life. Your boyfriend. Whatever you want to call it."

I furrowed my brow, feeling skeptical. "You never had a first chance. We just got hot and heavy out of nowhere on Christmas."

"Give me my first chance, then."

"Beau, it's not"

He put up a palm. "Let's skip this part. We both know it's not a good idea. We both know how things could go wrong. But you're in my heart, Shelby. You became someone important to me without either of us realizing it was happening. I think about you all the time. And don't tell me you're happier alone, because that's bullshit."

"You know this is crazy, right? You know I'm a complete introvert and you're the opposite. You're famous and I'm a hermit."

"I didn't choose to be famous; I just chose to play hockey. And who gives a shit? Yin and yang, right? Just stop being so damn stubborn for once and admit you want this, too."

"I mean, it's terrifying in every possible way, but...I think I do."

He pulled into the parking lot of the restaurant we were having dinner at and parked, then looked at me with the grin that rendered me powerless. Leaning over, he cupped my face in his hands and kissed me lightly.

"It's official then." He arched a brow. "Stop giving me that scrunched-up face."

"I can't see my face, but okay."

"When I hold your hand or I'm affectionate in public, people might take pictures of us. Those pictures might show up online."

I cringed.

"Just don't look at that bullshit and you won't have to worry about it. But when people find out who you are, there are going to be questions. That's just part of it, but since it's not my fault, you can't use it as a bullshit reason not to be with me."

I huffed a laugh. "Oh really?"

"Really."

"Well, since I'm obviously pregnant, maybe you should talk to your family."

That sobered him up fast. "Yeah, I need to."

"We have to talk about things some more. I may need to make a list about mutual expectations."

He laughed heartily. "An addendum for your binder?"

"Possibly."

"Whatever you need, Sunshine."

My gaze snapped to his in an instant. "What did you just call me?"

"Sunshine."

"But why?"

"Because you try so hard to be overcast sometimes, but the sun shines through, anyway. It's one of my favorite things about you."

He'd called me by my grandpa's nickname for my grandma without even realizing it. Though I was a practical, glass-half-empty sort of person, that got to me.

Coincidence? Maybe. But also, maybe not.

CHAPTER NINETEEN

Shelby

"Your bed isn't just firm, it's like a rock," I said. "Did you know you can sleep on the ground for free?"

"Firm mattresses are better for your back," Beau said. "Do I dare ask how you slept?"

"So hard. I don't even remember coming in here last night. I was watching a movie with you on the couch and then I woke up here a few minutes ago."

He grinned. "I carried you in here after you passed out so I wouldn't have to listen to you snoring anymore."

"Seriously?"

He furrowed his brow. "On which? The carrying or the snoring?"

"The carrying, of course. I'm basically two people right now."

"Well, I managed. Obviously."

Last night had been our second official date. After our first date, which was a long dinner at an upscale Italian place that I was seriously underdressed for, Beau had taken me home, kissed me at my door and left.

We'd had to wait a few days to get in another date, which had ended up being yesterday, Sunday night. I'd taken a half day off work today because I had an appointment with my OB-GYN later this morning.

"I can't believe I fell asleep and never woke up," I said, sitting up in bed.

"It's the mattress. You should dump your shitty, lumpy one."

"I do not have a lumpy mattress. You've never even laid on it."

His eyes sparkled with amusement. "I put my knee on it, though. I could tell it was lumpy."

"You're cuter when you don't talk."

He laughed and sat up in bed, and I saw that he was wearing nothing but boxers. A whole night next to him like that and I'd slept. Ridiculous.

"Well, you'll be happy to know my mouth will soon be…indisposed."

Alarm bells went off in my head. Did he mean what I thought he meant?

He slid my shirt up, exposing my giant belly, and then he kissed it, starting with my belly button and then glancing up at me before kissing it several more times, each kiss in a different spot.

I ran my fingers through his hair, my throat tightening with emotion over his affection toward our baby.

My baby. But also ours. This wasn't a good time for thinking. He was easing my elastic waistband pants down and I squirmed away, excited and overwhelmed at the same time.

"Hey, I haven't"

"Just relax and trust me," he said, gently placing his hands on my hips.

My inner cynic was in an uproar. I'd meant to schedule an appointment to get trimmed and waxed down there, but I hadn't yet. I'd also never let a man go down on me, and I didn't see how I'd survive letting Beau do this in broad daylight.

I pressed my lips together, trying to relax as he tugged my pants—and panties—down and off.

Holy crap. My vagina was completely exposed. Not that I could see it with my mountainous belly in the way. I squeezed my eyes closed, fighting the urge to kick him away.

"I knew you'd be this beautiful," he murmured, his lips grazing across my inner thigh. "I'm going to make this pussy mine, Shelby."

Oh. God. His words, and the way he was kissing his way up my thigh, so close to my core, made my back arch and my hand tighten in his hair.

"Pull hard when you like what I'm doing, baby," he said. "And make some noise for me."

Make some noise? Was I supposed to moan like women did in movies? I wasn't sure how to make a moan sound sexy. But when he ran the tip of his tongue up and down my slit, I couldn't manage to think of anything anymore.

"Oh, mmmah. Oh god, are you...ohhhh."

I didn't have any control over what I was saying. Sounds poured out of me as he swirled his tongue around my clit. Every stroke sent a jolt of electricity all the way down to the tips of my toes.

It was incredible. I no longer cared that it was my first time, or that I had a full bush down there. I just wanted more. Moaning and moving my hips in time with his mouth, I pulled on his hair, feeling myself climbing higher toward climax.

He wasn't going to have any hair left by the time he finished. It would be worth it, though.

"Don't stop," I panted. "Please don't stop doing that, oh my god."

He stopped. I looked up, shocked, confused, and frustrated.

"What? No!"

He scrambled to his feet and pushed down his boxers, his erection jutting out toward me. And holy wow, was it impressive.

"I want to be inside you when you come for the first time with me," he said, his eyes glazed with lust. "Trust me, you'll enjoy it more this way."

I nodded and he came back to bed, untying the ribbon below my breasts on my maternity top. Together, we got my shirt off and then he unclasped my bra. I was still pulsing with need for him, the sensation heightened when he took each of my nipples in his mouth, sucking and licking each one until I was moaning again, my hand snaking back into his hair.

"Tell me if you want me to stop," he said.

"I will."

He kissed me gently, his eyes on mine as he got to his knees and put a pillow beneath my bottom.

"Go slowly," I said.

"I promise I will."

He slid a couple of inches into me, and it was bliss. As he eased farther in, he put his thumb on my clit, circling it. It was all I could focus on. I didn't tense up as he went deeper.

"Christ." His voice was strained. "Your pussy is so tight. Feels fucking amazing."

I rocked my hips up, desperate for him to increase the pressure on my clit.

"I wish you could see how sexy you look right now," he said, pulling out and then slowly thrusting back in. "Taking almost my whole cock in that virgin pussy. I'm gonna come so hard in this sweet pussy, but not until you come first."

Now I understood all the hype about sex. The way he felt thrusting in and out of me and groaning like that was enough to undo me. Add in his attention to my clit and I was climbing toward a climax harder than I'd ever felt.

He slowed his fingers, lightening the pressure until I groaned with frustration.

"You want me to get this sweet little pussy off?" he ground out. "You have to talk to me, baby."

"Yes," I begged, desperation in my tone. "Please don't stop. Make me come."

He was thrusting harder and faster now, grunting with the strain of holding back.

"You've got my whole cock now, baby," he said gruffly. "Every inch of me buried in your pussy. I've waited a long time for this pussy and I plan to enjoy it now. I didn't want anyone but you, you know that, right? No one else since the day we met."

"Oh god." He was circling faster now, giving me exactly the right amount of pressure. "Beau, I'm going to come."

"God*damn*, babe. Say my name again."

"Beau…please don't stop."

I fell apart, shattering into a million pieces, overcome with sensation. He was right behind me, coming with a guttural groan. As I came down from the high, I felt the discomfort my body had been too turned on to notice earlier, and I inhaled sharply.

He gently pulled out of me and lay beside me, brushing the hair from my forehead.

"You okay?" he asked.

I smiled. "I'm better than okay. I was so sure it would hurt, but you made it so good."

He kissed my forehead. "Arousal masks pain pretty well."

"Wow. Is that why people don't mind getting flogged during sex?"

With an amused smile, he said, "Must be, but I've never done that."

"I'm really sorry to do this right now, but do you know where my phone is? I need to look something up."

"I put it on the nightstand on your side. Everything okay?"

I grabbed my phone, entered the passcode, and quickly googled *can babies feel sex*.

"Okay, good," I said, relieved. "Sex makes the uterus contract, and the baby might be able to feel that, but it's not a big deal."

He arched a brow, grinning. "You just checked to see if the baby knew we were having sex?"

"I mean...yeah."

"You worried the kid's gonna come out with a look of judgment and tell all the doctors and nurses his parents boned?"

"His *or* her."

"Right." His expression had turned serious. "I want to be there when our baby is born. And after, too. You know that, right?"

I nodded, a lump in my throat.

"Is that okay?" he asked.

I pulled the covers over myself, suddenly shy now that we were talking about something other than sex.

"I've thought about it a lot," I said. "And it's okay, but I want to be honest with you that it scares me. It's one of the reasons I was hesitant to get involved with you."

He pushed his brows together in a concerned look. "I don't understand."

"If things don't work out with us, you could end up married with other kids later, and our child would probably prefer the life you can give them over what I have to offer."

"Hey," he said softly, sitting up on an elbow. "Kids don't think like that, and I'd never, ever try to take this baby from you. You have my word."

I nodded, grateful for his reassurance.

"And another thing," he said, his lips quirking up in a smile, "Why are you assuming things won't work between us? The past couple of weeks have been great, haven't they?"

"Yeah." I reached my hand into his hair and gently ran my fingers through it. It always felt so soft. "I'm happy. Very happy. But life has pulled the rug out from under me in the past, and I've learned to be prepared."

"Being prepared is one thing, but you expect people to fail you."

He put an arm out, a silent invite for me to snuggle against his chest. As soon as my cheek reached his warm skin, I closed my eyes, reveling in the sensation. This was quickly becoming my favorite place to be. He put his arm around my back and kissed the top of my head.

"Has anyone ever failed you?" I asked him.

"Yeah." He traced a fingertip down the length of my spine. "I had a girlfriend when I was in the minors. I was crazy about her. I was saving up for an engagement ring. I came home early one day and found her in our bed with my best friend."

"How horrible. I'm so sorry."

He grunted dismissively. "I thought catching them was the worst thing that had ever happened to me, but it turned out to be the best. I dodged two bullets. Never spoke to either of them again. Fiona went over there while my ex moved her stuff out, and that was it."

I'd been wrong to assume that because Beau was wealthy, attractive, and had a great family, he'd never been hurt. He'd been betrayed, but he hadn't let it darken his spirit.

"I'll try," I said softly. "Not to assume the worst, I mean. To hope that things will turn out okay."

"I'm glad to hear it." He ran his palm down to the small of my back. "And I'm also going to try."

"Try what?"

"To get you off again by finishing what I started earlier. Get on your back, Sunshine."

CHAPTER TWENTY

Shelby

"THE CRIB IS ASSEMBLED," Beau said, walking into my living room. "And I need a beer."

I kept my gaze focused on the computer screen as I responded, because I was trying to stay focused on work even though he was at my apartment at two in the afternoon on a weekday.

"I thought a fight was about to break out between you and the crib there for a little bit."

"Those fucking instructions were bullshit. Completely counterintuitive. I had it halfway assembled and then I had to take it all the way apart and start over."

I saved the document I was working on, which

was a scintillating summary of two weeks' worth of eminent domain research and turned to him.

"I'll be honest, it's nice to know you're mortal and there are things that make you crazy. You're usually Mr. Cool."

"Mr. Cool, huh?" He grinned as he put everything back into the toolbox he'd brought over to assemble baby furniture. "Right now I'm more like Mr. Horny. Is your boss nice enough to let you take a break?"

I flushed at the thought of an afternoon quickie, and the feelings that Beau could bring on with just a few simple words. Or a meaningful look. Sometimes a text. This was what it was like to fall hard for someone—you willingly, giddily ceded your control to them. Marlowe said I had heart eyes twenty-four seven now.

It had been almost two weeks since Beau and I officially became a couple. I was still scared, because he was going to be part of our baby's life. But the more time I spent sitting with my feelings and really thinking about them, the more I came to realize that was actually a good thing.

I'd chosen Beau as my baby's father because of how great he was on paper, but I'd since found out he was also amazing in all the intangible ways you can't discover until you truly know someone.

He loved his family and his teammates. He

jumped in to help when someone needed it. Unless he was assembling furniture, he was easygoing and always had a smile.

Some of the fears and feelings I'd confronted since meeting Beau weren't pleasant, but there had also been joy, longing, and hope. For so long, I'd tried to protect myself against feeling anything. That had led to a lonely life, though, and I didn't want to force my own anxieties on my child.

"My boss is pretty amazing," I said as Beau walked over to me, his eyes swimming with hunger. "She'd be okay with a break."

"Does your boss look as sexy as you do in glasses?"

I straightened my dark-framed glasses and pretended to consider his question. "Oddly, she looks almost exactly like I do in glasses."

He turned my desk chair so I was facing him, putting a hand on each chair arm and leaning down to kiss me softly.

"My library books are all overdue," he murmured against my lips. "And I've bent the corners of the pages on all of them."

"Oh, that will not do," I said, playing along. "You've disappointed your librarian, Mr. Fox. What am I going to do with you?"

His mouth found mine again, the kiss full of

pent-up sexual energy. No matter how many times we had sex in every position that accommodated my belly, it was never enough.

"I'm willing to work off my transgressions," he said in a low tone. "Maybe"

Our moment of bliss was interrupted by a knock at the door. Beau sighed.

"Marlowe has the worst timing. Let's pretend we're not here. Where were we?"

"I can't pretend to not be here, silly. She knows I work from home and our cars are in the parking lot."

He furrowed his brow and made a growly sound. "She'll get the hint and assume we're in bed. And we will be in about thirty seconds."

I moaned softly as he kissed my neck, which was my weakness. The knock sounded again, but this time it was longer and louder.

"Hey, that's not Marlowe's knock," I said. "And she wouldn't come over while she thinks I'm working, anyway."

He groaned. "Okay, okay. The cockblocker wins."

I laughed as he moved away from my chair and I stood up. "Hey, you do realize this is probably a delivery or something and we can carry on in like one minute, right?"

"Can I get that in writing?"

Shaking my head at him, I opened the door

expecting to find a postal carrier, but it was my mom standing there. She didn't look as bad as she did last time, but her hair still hadn't been fixed. Now she had three-inch roots and it didn't look like her hair had been brushed in a while.

"Hi," she said, smiling brightly.

My heart hammered in my chest, everything I felt when I found her and my stuff gone on New Year's Day rushing back at once. The pain of that day hit so hard, I felt like I'd been punched.

"What are you doing here?" I demanded.

"I know you're mad," she said, reaching into her purse. "But Shelby, you have to understand that I was in a bad situation. I brought you this."

She held out some folded bills and I looked down at the money and then up at her. "What is that for?"

"You know, to make up for what I borrowed."

I put a hand on the doorframe to steady myself, so angry I was getting light-headed. "You didn't borrow anything from me, you stole it. How much money is that?"

"It's a hundred dollars."

I laughed, on the verge of crying with frustration. "It cost me more than two grand to get my stuff back. And that was after calling pawnshops for more than two hours to find it."

"Look, I'm sorry," she said, sounding agitated.

"I'm trying to make it right." Her gaze moved down to my belly. "Oh my god, you're pregnant."

"What do you want?" I asked again.

"I want you to take this money." She moved her hand closer to me. "I'll get you the rest, but I just need some time."

"I don't want the money. Is there anything else?"

She exhaled heavily, getting more and more irritated that I wouldn't accept her offer. "Aren't you going to let me in?"

Like last time, I was torn. She wouldn't be here if she had other options, and I wasn't heartless. But I couldn't trust her, and I wouldn't have peace if she was in my home again.

"Why would I let you in after you stole from me?" I asked, on the verge of breaking down.

"I said I was sorry."

"That doesn't make it okay. And why are you sorry now, all these months later?"

Her eyes filled with shame and she looked at the ground. Standing up to her was agonizing. Terrifying. I'd never done it before.

"What do you want me to do?" she said bitterly. "I got kicked out of the place I was staying. I don't have anywhere to go."

I heard Beau approaching, and then felt his hand on my back. He opened the door a little wider to stand next to me. My mom looked from him back to me.

"Who's that?"

"I'm Beau. Shelby's boyfriend."

My mom transformed, putting on her most winning smile. "A boyfriend? Are you the baby's father?"

I cut in. "It's none of your business."

She recoiled. "My grandchild is none of my business? Why are you being so hurtful, Shelby?"

Beau rubbed small, reassuring circles on my back as he spoke to my mom. "You can't stay here. I'll gladly drive you to the hospital if you want to get checked in for some help, or I'll take you to a homeless shelter."

"A homeless shelter? I'm not homeless, and I don't need a hospital," she said indignantly. "Whatever you've done to my daughter, I don't like it." She looked directly at me. "Shelby, you need to ask him to leave."

I knew she wasn't a good mother. She'd neglected me as a child, always put herself first, and showed no interest in me for years once I'd moved in with my grandparents. She'd stolen from me. But still, this confrontation hurt me in a deep way I had no control over.

"I'm not leaving," Beau said.

My mom took out an old flip-style cell phone. "Well, let's see what the police have to say about that."

"No," I said, panic filling my chest.

Beau slid his hand to my hip, pulling me a little closer to him. "If she wants to call, let her. The police will help her if you tell them her situation."

My mom's eyes darkened. "What situation? What did you tell him?"

"The truth," I said, feeling weary. "That you're bipolar but you don't take your meds like you're supposed to."

"I'm not falling into that trap by the drug companies," she said, her tone laced with scorn. "They make people think they need those overpriced drugs but it's all just a scam."

"Mom, you're better when you're on your meds. I wouldn't tell you that if it wasn't the truth."

She shook her head, stuffing the cash back into her handbag. "Yes, you would. You'd say anything to get me to go along with the doctors. You want them to lock me up again. I don't know why I thought you'd help me. You've always been a selfish brat."

Beau looked down at me. "Go lock yourself in the bedroom. I'll handle this."

"You don't have to." I was shaking, already letting her words break me.

"Go. Please."

I nodded and walked away, my mom yelling my name. I squeezed my eyes shut and forced myself to keep going.

"Move back," Beau said firmly. "You're not getting through this doorway."

"That's my daughter! Don't you dare touch me, you bastard." She screamed and I heard a scuffle that sounded like her pounding her fists on his chest.

"I'm not touching you, but I'm not moving from the doorway. You need to go or I'll call the police."

"Shelby! Shelby!"

I put a hand on my belly, rubbing it as I walked into my bedroom, closed the door, and locked it. Closing my eyes, I sat on the edge of my bed and cried, making myself breathe in and out. After a couple of minutes, there was a soft knock on the door.

"Hey," Beau said. "Can I come in?"

Silently, I got up and walked to the door to unlock it and open it. As soon as I did, he put his arms around me and I relaxed into him, emotionally worn out.

"You did the right thing," he said. "There are places she can go for help."

"I know," I said through my tears.

"It still hurts, though."

I nodded as he rubbed my back and kissed the top of my head. Turning her away had been every bit as painful as finding out she'd stolen from me, but this time was different.

This time, I didn't have to go through it alone.

CHAPTER TWENTY-ONE

Shelby

"Almost!" Marlowe ran over to her phone and stopped the video she was recording.

"Ugh, I'm hopeless. You should just do it by yourself."

"No way, TikTok dances are for at least two people."

I scoffed. "I *am* two people right now. I'm also thirty-five weeks pregnant and deeply uncoordinated. Where are the Doritos?"

She grinned and set the camera back up in the spot she'd been using to record us doing this dance for half an hour now. It had taken me an hour just to learn it and I was ready to throw in the towel.

"I happen to have a brand-new bag of spicy Doritos stashed in my kitchen for you."

"Unopened?" My commitment to quitting wavered.

"Yep. You know how much you love that first chip out of the bag. All fresh and spicy and delicious."

"It's the baby who loves it. You're denying the baby food over this dance."

She laughed. "It'll be worth it, I promise. You're the cutest thing I've ever seen dancing with your Buddha belly."

"Fine," I said, scowling. "But after this, Doritos."

Trying to get the dance right was a good distraction from the false contractions I'd been having. I'd grabbed my hospital bag and driven myself to the hospital yesterday, convinced I was in labor. Then I'd driven myself back home a couple of hours later, defeated and feeling like a dumbass.

I just hoped I wouldn't have five weeks of false labor contractions until my due date. It was hard to focus on anything but the discomfort. Fortunately, it was Saturday and I was off work. Beau had a game at home tonight that Marlowe and I were planning to watch on TV.

He'd invited us to go in person, and we had planned to go, but now I wasn't up for it because I was uncomfortable, and I didn't think I'd fit well in an arena seat at my current size.

Marlowe started the music on her phone—"Uptown Funk" —and we both watched the timer on her phone counting down. As soon as it started recording, we busted out the moves we'd been practicing. I concentrated on every move, motivated entirely by being done with this so I could sit down on Marlowe's couch with the Doritos I'd been promised.

We were just a few seconds from nailing the dance from start to finish when I felt a warm gushing between my legs. Water poured onto the floor between my feet and I shot Marlowe a panicked look.

"Oh my god!" I cried. "Did my water just break? What's happening?"

Her eyes were round. "Okay, uh…don't panic. Should I call an ambulance?"

"I don't know! I'm supposed to be in false labor!"

"I'll google it!" She lunged for her phone.

"I need to get to the hospital," I said, doubling over from a sudden shot of pain. "Holy hell, this hurts."

"The hospital!" She looked up from her phone. "We need to get you to the hospital. Where are my keys?"

"You can drive my car," I said, groaning in pain. "I don't want to get...birth fluids all over your car interior."

"Mine's parked closer; we're taking it."

I cried out as a contraction gripped me. "Marlowe, what's happening? Am I in labor?"

"Based on watching every episode of *Grey's Anatomy*, I think so."

"No," I wailed. "This is supposed to happen at the hospital."

"Let's go, mama. Be strong for your baby."

She put an arm around me and I took a deep breath as we moved toward her front door. I had to be strong, like she said. The faster we got to the hospital, the safer my delivery would be.

We made it halfway down the stairs when I stopped, gripping the handrail for dear life as I breathed through another contraction. I'd never experienced pain like this. Marlowe waited until I was able to move again, and then we made it the rest of the way down the stairs.

"My phone," I said as we neared the door to my apartment. "Where's my phone?"

"I have it. I put your phone and keys in my bag before we left my apartment."

"I need my phone."

"So you can post our dance video?" she cracked.

I glowered at her, in no mood for jokes.

"Tough crowd," she said, reaching into her bag for my phone and passing it to me.

I dialed Beau's number as we slowly walked toward Marlowe's little electric car. Another contraction was hitting when I got his voice mail.

"Hey, it's Beau. You know what to do."

"Beau, it's…oh my god, that hurts." I paused to breathe in and out a couple of times. "I'm in labor. Marlowe is"—another breath—" taking me to the hospital. You know which one."

Marlowe took my phone and I grimaced as she opened the passenger door to her car.

"It's so tiny, and I'm so huge."

"Get in before the next contraction hits. Unless you want to have your baby in this parking lot?"

I groaned and folded myself into her car, grateful she'd taken charge. This was not part of my birth plan. I had a bag inside with the music I wanted to listen to, clothes for me and the baby, and my written wishes for the birth.

There was no time to get the bag, though. This baby was coming five weeks early. I tried not to scream as Marlowe drove, another contraction striking.

"The hospital isn't far; hang in there," she said,

running a red light. "I'm pretty sure that light was pink."

"God, it's like someone's trying to murder me from the inside," I said, whimpering. "I thought I'd be all breathing and finding my zen but this is some bullshit."

"I can see the hospital sign. We're almost there, Shelby."

"Don't leave me alone," I begged. "Will you stay until Beau comes?"

"Bitch, I'm not going anywhere. You're my best friend and I'm not leaving you when you're in labor."

Another contraction hit, and it was the worst one yet. I was screaming as Marlowe pulled into the ER entrance turnaround, stopping under the big portico and running around to help me out of the car.

"Help!" she yelled. "She's having a baby!"

———

"SHELBY, I need you to push now," the doctor said, looking up from between my legs.

"Come on, mama," Marlowe said, putting an arm behind my neck and holding my hand with her other one. "You can do this. It's almost time to meet your baby."

"Where's Beau?" I asked her. "Did he call back?"

"I haven't looked. I'm kind of in the middle of something here. Listen to the doctor and push."

I leaned up on my elbows and gave it everything I had, collapsing back onto the bed when the doctor said I could take a break.

"Where is he?" I wondered out loud. "He's not traveling or anything and he said he'd keep his phone on him all the time."

"Okay, time to push again," the doctor said. "I can see the baby's head. There's a lot of dark hair."

My baby had dark hair, just like Beau. I took a deep breath and pushed as hard as I could, the pain still intense. I'd have my child in my arms soon. A child I'd love until my dying breath.

"Here we go. Another big push, Shelby," the doctor said.

"Come on, you've got this," one of the nurses said in encouragement.

I pushed with every ounce of strength in me, feeling like I was being torn in two.

"The head is out," the doctor said. "Stop pushing for just a second."

I panted like I'd learned in my birthing class, fighting my urge to push. The doctor gave me an encouraging look and said, "Okay, another big push."

I pushed, yelling at the top of my lungs as the pain got worse and then suddenly better.

"What's happening?" I asked Marlowe, my body going limp.

She squeezed my hand and watched the doctor working. "I don't know. Keep breathing."

Dread filled my chest. The baby was out, but there was no crying. I looked at Marlowe frantically just as a high wail filled the room.

"Shelby, you have a beautiful baby boy," the doctor said, holding up my baby so I could see him.

I burst into tears of joy. My son. I'd dreamed of this moment.

"I love you," I said to him, my head dropping to the bed.

"Five pounds, two ounces," a nurse announced. "We'll have him over to you very soon, Mom."

I tried to compose myself as they swaddled him in a blanket and put a little cap on his head. Once they put him in my arms, though, I lost it again. Marlowe was beside the bed, snapping photo after photo of us.

"Your name is Charlie," I said, looking into his wrinkled, red face. "After your great grandpa."

The nurses helped me try to nurse him, but he didn't latch on. They assured me it was okay and we'd try again later.

"Do you want to hold him?" I asked Marlowe. "I'm hoping you'll be his godmother."

"Me?" Her eyes filled with tears. "Of course I will."

She reached over and gently took the bundle that was Charlie from my arms.

"Oh, Shelby, you did good. He's perfect."

"Let me take a picture of you with him."

She handed me her phone and posed with my newborn son, and my heart filled with love for them both. It would have been the perfect moment, if Beau were here, too.

"Has he called?" I asked Marlowe.

Knowing who I meant, she walked over to check my phone, which was in her bag. She shook her head and I sighed softly. Either something was wrong, or Beau had changed his mind and bailed. Both options made me feel physically ill.

"Hey, stay in this moment," Marlowe said gently. "This is one of the most joyful days you'll ever have."

I nodded, knowing she was right. Charlie deserved all my attention.

"I'm going to try nursing him again," I said.

A nurse walked in and saw me untying my hospital gown.

"We'll have to wait just a few minutes for that," she said. "We need to move you up to OB right away because we have a lot of patients coming in from a big explosion downtown. They'll get you cleaned up and into a nursing gown, and it's a lot quieter up there, too."

She used her foot to switch off the brake on my hospital bed. We were still on the emergency floor. I'd been too far along in my labor to be taken up to the obstetrics floor when I arrived. I turned to look at her, my heart racing.

"An explosion downtown?" I asked. "Where was it?"

"The Shapiro Center. Where the Coyotes play. Apparently, there's supposed to be a home game there tonight and there were a lot of people there."

I held on to Charlie, tears streaming down my cheeks as she wheeled me out of the room.

CHAPTER TWENTY-TWO

Beau

WHEN I COUGHED, my chest hurt and my mouth felt gritty. All I could taste was…dust? Where the hell was I? Everything felt foggy and when I tried to move, my body felt like it was stuck in quicksand.

Water. I needed water. I blinked, the air around me clouded by debris that seemed to be everywhere.

I coughed some more, unable to stop myself even though it made my body ache. Somewhere in the middle of my coughing fit, I finally remembered where I was.

I was at the arena, and I'd been on my way from the locker room to my car, because I'd just gotten a message that Shelby was in labor. Out of nowhere, something terrible had obviously happened, and I felt a deep, desperate need to get out of there.

My best guess was that the building had partially collapsed. There were chunks of concrete piled around me. I had to fight through the pain and was barely able to maneuver my body into a standing position. By the time I made it to my knees, I was gassed. I bent over and coughed more, then spit the collective dust from inside my mouth.

I was okay. Sore all over, but able to get up. What about everyone else, though? It was dark and I couldn't see through the wreckage in front of me, so I reached out my hands and moved over the piles of debris until I found a wall.

"Hello?" I called out, the single word sending me into another coughing fit. "Can anyone hear me?"

Nothing. I slowly moved in the direction I thought was the locker room. I had nothing but instinct to go on and I wasn't sure what direction I was going.

"Hey!" I yelled as loudly as I could. "Is anyone there?"

My pulse pounded as I made my way through the rubble, the wall I had my hand on ending with broken pieces of what felt like brick. Whatever had happened, there were a lot of people in here when it went down. My teammates and coaches, a lot of arena staff, the team we were playing tonight… hundreds of people were here. Fuck. It was naive to hope everyone was okay.

At this point, I wasn't even sure I was going to get out of here. The whole building could come down at any moment. Shelby was at the hospital delivering our baby, and I was missing it. I might never see her again and I might never meet our child.

As I stumbled over the debris, I took my cell phone from my pocket. I was a dipshit—a call to 911 should have been my first move.

I couldn't see it through the haze in the air, but I felt the smashed remnants of my phone, and my panic skyrocketed. I had to get the hell out of hereI'd crawl if I had to.

Slowly and steadily, I made my way through the rubble, yelling every fifteen seconds or so in case anyone else was in my path. A weak cry for help made me stop cold.

"Hello?" I yelled. "It's Beau Fox. I can hear you, but I need you to keep making noise so I can get to you."

"Help me." The voice sounded choked.

I got down on my hands and knees, which was painful but allowed me to move faster.

"Help me! I'm bleeding," the voice called out.

It was a woman, and she sounded like she hardly had the energy to speak. Finally, I reached her, my hands moving all over the blocks of concrete on the ground until they found something warm.

"What's your name?" I asked, knowing I needed to keep her with me.

"Andie. I'm an usher."

"Andie, I'm Beau." I found what felt like her arm and moved down along the length of it until I got to her hand.

"Don't leave me here," she begged, coughing through the words. "I don't want to die."

"I'm not leaving you," I said, picking up a chunk of concrete and throwing it aside. "We're going to get out of here together. Stay with me."

One broken block at a time, I moved the pieces of concrete pinning her in place.

"Tell me what hurts the most," I said as I worked, breathing hard.

"My..." She stopped to cough. "Foot and ankle. And my chest."

Instinct had kicked in; I was focused entirely on getting this woman out of here safely.

"I want you to try to move parts of your body as I uncover them," I said, wiping sweat from my brow with the back of my hand. "Tell me if you can't move anything."

"Okay…my right arm is okay. My neck is okay." I felt her squirming. "I'm close to getting my left arm out. I can"—she stopped and coughed, long and hard—"almost sit up. I just coughed up something…tastes like blood."

Shit. I doubled down, determined to get her unburied, and she howled with pain when I uncovered her left foot.

The dust was finally settling, and from what I could see of her left foot and ankle, she was definitely not walking out of here. There was a lot of blood. I blew out a breath and found one of her hands, holding on to it as I spoke.

"I'm going to level with you. Your left foot and ankle are completely crushed. The damage is really bad."

She started crying. "Don't leave me here. Please."

The weight of whatever had happened to the arena settled in my chest like a lead ball. Were my teammates buried in what was left of this building, too? Or worse? I had to focus on what I could control in this moment, which was getting Andie out of here.

"I won't leave you. I promise. But we've got a situation here. I can't carry you because there are piles of concrete all over the place and I don't want to slip and drop you. I'm going to try putting you on my back and crawling until we find a place I can pick you up safely, and it's going to hurt like hell having your foot flopping around."

"Do it," she said.

She shouted out in pain as I tried to move her onto my back, and she held on around my neck but kept sliding off of me, inadvertently choking me.

"Sorry," she said, her tone panicked.

"It's okay. We'll get there."

We were trying to get her onto my back once more when a massive boom sounded and the ground beneath us started shaking.

"Oh shit," Andie wailed. "Is it an earthquake?"

Whatever it was, I was pretty sure it had damaged the arena further. With every passing second, I realized we might not make it out of here alive.

"New plan," I said. "Let go of my neck. I'm just going to carry you."

"Okay."

She screamed as she hit the ground, her foot hurting more than I could even imagine. I gritted my teeth and stood, scooping her into my arms and holding her against me as I picked my way over the debris on the ground, slipping and stumbling, but somehow keeping my balance.

"I know where we are," she said suddenly.

"There's a *D* on the wall there. That means there's an exit ahead."

Every muscle in my body ached and it was hard to breathe. One foot at a time, I moved forward.

"Hey!" a male voice called to us. "Hey, who's there?"

Several people were running toward us from a hallway off of the main basement tunnel, which was where we were.

"Beau Fox," I said, grateful everyone coming toward us was upright, because I couldn't have carried anyone else. "And Andie."

"Beau, it's Greg Carver from the front office. And I've got a few people here with me. Are you guys okay?"

As he approached us, I saw that he and the others with him were okay. They weren't covered in dust, cuts, and bruises like me and Andie.

"She needs medical attention right now," I said, looking down at her foot, which was a mangled mess dripping blood.

"Oh shit," Greg said. "There's an exit close by; that's where we're going. You want me to see if I can take her from you?"

"No, just get us to the door."

He nodded and clapped my shoulder as he ran ahead, and I winced in pain. I followed, Andie's shallow breathing making me move faster than I should have been able to.

Finally, I saw the rectangle of artificial light around the open doorway, from the light fixtures inside the arena where the stairs and elevator were located. Once through it, we went to the stairs and I summoned every ounce of will I had to walk up them. There was a door at the top, sunlight beckoning me to keep going as Greg held it open.

I stopped once we were outside, trying desperately to catch my breath. Greg's eyes were wide as he looked up at us from his phone screen.

"We have to keep going," he said. "They think it was an explosion, and there could be more."

That's what the second boom had beenanother explosion. I locked eyes with Greg.

"You take her," I said. "I'm going back in."

"Beau, you can't. It's not safe."

Safe or not, I was going back in. There were many people in that arena who would do the same for me.

"My teammates are in there. Take her."

"We need to let the professionals handle it," Greg said, his tone indicating that it was somehow his decision to make.

I was about to lose my shit. Every second he

argued with me was time lost. I held Andie out toward him.

"She needs help right now. Take her."

With a resigned look, he put his arms out and I passed Andie to him.

"If I don't make it out, tell Shelby I love her and I want her to have an amazing life," I said, my throat tight. "Promise me."

"I promise."

Damn. I hoped that wasn't the last thing I'd ever get to tell Shelby. I wanted to tell her myself that I loved her. I wanted to meet our baby and see him or her grow up.

Him. My gut told me we were having a son.

I turned to go back through the door we'd come out of.

"Beau, be careful!" Greg called after me.

I waved over my shoulder, finding the door locked and kicking it out of frustration. There were many other doors that led into the arena, though. I'd find one, get back in, and find my teammates.

I'll get to them, I told myself. *I'll find a way.* There was no other option.

CHAPTER TWENTY-THREE

Shelby

"Look at the way he's looking at you," Claire Fox said, sitting beside my hospital bed as Charlie nursed. "He knows you're his mama."

I smiled down at my son. "I never could have imagined how emotional it would be to breastfeed him. I'm glad we finally got him to latch."

"Is there anything you need?"

"If you could hold him when he finishes eating, that would be great. My arms are feeling tired."

She stroked a hand over my hair, the tender gesture making tears well in my eyes. "Of course I will. And when you get out of the hospital, Henry and I are here for you and Charlie and Beau."

"Has Henry said anything else?" I asked her.

She checked her phone. "No. I'll text and ask if there are any updates."

The entire Fox family had come to the hospital when they heard about the accident. Beau had called his parents when he was being brought to the hospital in an ambulance and asked them to come here to be with me and the baby, if I'd delivered.

Things were chaotic for an hour or so, Beau's family members taking turns checking on him in the ER and me on the OB floor. They'd all assured me he was stable and pleading with the doctors to let him come up to my room to see me and Charlie.

I wouldn't be able to relax fully until I saw him with my own eyes. He had broken ribs and several cuts and bruises but was otherwise okay. The ER was so backed up with patients from the arena explosion that it was taking a long time for them to get Beau cleaned up.

"Do the police know what happened?" I asked Claire.

Her expression turned grim. "They think it was intentional. Two bombs placed in the area, but it'll take a full investigation before they announce much more. I work with a woman whose son is a fire inspector, and he apparently told her the arena will have to be torn down."

Charlie was asleep, his little belly full of milk, his tiny mouth hanging open. I used a cloth to dab the milk from the corner of his mouth and then passed him to his grandma.

"Did they get everyone out?" I asked.

"Sadly, probably not," she said, settling Charlie into her arms. "They aren't releasing any numbers until tomorrow."

"My god." I sat back against my inclined bed, the gravity of it all bringing tears to my eyes. "Beau's whole team was probably in there."

Claire rocked Charlie in her arms, smiling sadly.

"It's not fair that this tragedy overshadowed such a happy day for you and Beau," she said. "He's so excited about the baby; it's all he's been talking about for weeks. Well, and you, of course. I've never seen him so happy. These next weeks and months are probably going to be hard for him, so I just ask that you try to give him grace. Beau has always been my drifter. Other than hockey, he just wanders from thing to thing and person to person, never really finding anything that captures his heart. Until you."

I wiped tears from my cheeks. "I'll do everything I can to support him. Beau is an extrovert and I'm an introvert, and I know I can come off as aloof and detached, but when I love someone, I love them hard."

She smiled and nodded. "Thank you, Shelby. And remember, Henry and I want to help with Charlie. If you and Beau want to stay with us for a while, we have plenty of room and we'd love to have you. But if not, that's okay, too. I know how hard it is to have a new baby."

My eyelids started drifting closed. "I can't believe how tired I am, and the hard work hasn't even started yet."

Claire chuckled. "I'd say delivering a baby is hard work. Try to get some sleep. I'll just sit in the rocker with Charlie."

I watched her as she rocked him and softly told him about all the adventures he'd have at Grandma and Grandpa's house when he was older, and peace settled over me.

My son would have what I never did as a child—a big, loving family to be his joy and his safe place. Knowing that healed part of the hurt I still carried around, though I knew some of the wounds from my childhood would always be there.

It was because of those wounds that I knew how precious my son was. Living years without a loving family made me appreciate the Foxesespecially Beauthat much more.

———

"Shelby."

I woke to Beau's voice, and when I opened my eyes, he was practically running toward me, tears welling in his eyes. Several cords dragged on the ground, like he'd ripped them out of the machines he was hooked up to and bolted.

"Hey," I said, sitting up and looking him over from head to toe as well as I could in the second it took him to get to my bedside. "You're here."

He leaned down and put his arms around me, cringing in pain and kissing me on the forehead at the same time.

I tilted my head up so I could see his face. He had a few small cuts on his cheeks, but his face was relatively unscathed. His hair had light-colored dust sprinkled in it and his right bicep had a bandage peeking out from beneath the sleeve of his hospital gown.

He was okay, though, and that meant I could fully breathe again.

"I love you," he said, cupping my face in his hands. "I wasn't sure I'd get the chance to tell you that. I'm sorry I wasn't here for you when you needed me, but I love you and the only thing that will ever keep me from you is being trapped in a collapsed building." His voice broke with emotion. "And even then, I'll find my way back to you."

He brushed a kiss over my lips and rested his forehead against mine. This was, without question, the most emotional, beautiful day of my life.

"I love you, too," I said. "And you don't need to be sorry. It was out of your control. I'm just so grateful you're okay. Are you sure it's okay that you're here?"

He shrugged. "No one's been in my room for forty-five minutes. Everyone's busy treating the people who were hurt worse than I was."

His expression had darkened, and I cradled his jaw in my hand, rubbing my thumb over his cheekbone. "I'm so sorry. Do you know if your teammates are okay?"

"I know of a few teammates who got out, but we still don't know about a lot of them."

He was emotionally wrecked—understandably. I didn't know exactly how to be there for him, but I'd figure it out. He'd been the one caring for me for much of the time we'd known each other, and I wanted to do the same for him.

"Keep the faith," I said, taking his hand. "That's all you can do right now."

Claire had told me there was a massive search and rescue effort underway at the arena. I was deliberately avoiding my phone because I wasn't ready to hear bad news about it.

"Meet your son," Claire said, walking over with our sleeping, silent baby. "This is Charlie."

Beau's face crumpled when he looked at him. He reached out and his mom gently passed Charlie to him, a nurse frantically trying to put a surgical cap over Beau's hair, probably because of the dust he still had in it.

"Charlie, I'm your dad," he said, crying.

I lost it, too. What a road we'd walked together since I'd asked him eight months ago to be my sperm donor. There had been so many surprises, including Charlie's early arrival.

"He's good?" Beau asked me, looking up to meet my gaze. "Even though he's five weeks early?"

"He's perfect."

Beau lowered his face to kiss our son's tiny forehead. "You're strong, Charlie. You're a Fox."

He seemed to remember at that moment that we'd never discussed Charlie's last name.

"Yes," I said softly. "And I want you to choose his middle name. Charlie was my grandpa's name. I hope that's okay with you."

"It's perfect. What about Charlie Grant Fox? That way he has your grandparents' last name in there, too."

I thought I'd cried all the tears I had today, but

that brought forth a few more. I nodded, incredibly grateful my intuition had told me this was the man who should be my baby's father.

"Hey, turn around so I can get a picture," Fiona said from behind Beau.

He moved and I realized almost the entire family was in the room. Claire stood next to Henry, both of them looking overjoyed. Asher, Chloe, and their kids stood together beneath the TV mounted to the ceiling. Fiona was there, minus Adrian and their new baby, and Isaac stood with her. Genevieve was the only sibling who wasn't here, since she was away at medical school.

Beau passed Charlie back to me and I settled him against my chest. Beau leaned close, smiling for a few pictures and then kissing me on the cheek for another.

"Welcome to the den, Shelby and Charlie," Fiona said.

Marlowe walked in then, carrying a tote with a bag of spicy Doritos poking out of the top.

"Beau, are you okay?" she asked as soon as she saw him.

"Yeah, I'm fine. I heard you took care of Shelby when she went into labor. I appreciate it."

She grinned. "Well, she's my best friend. And it's

not every day she goes into labor while we're recording a TikTok dance."

Beau gave me a shocked look. "*You* were doing a TikTok dance?"

"I was bribed with Doritos."

"Check it out," Marlowe said, holding her phone out for Beau to see the screen. "It already has more than 10,000 views."

I groaned as I listened to myself realizing my water had just broken. Marlowe hadn't told me she was posting it, but I wasn't surprised.

Beau smiled at me, his eyes dancing with happiness. "That's the best TikTok I've ever seen."

"I love it," Fiona said. "You're a total rock star, Shelby."

I realized Marlowe hadn't been introduced to almost everyone in the room.

"Marlowe, this is Beau's family. Everyone, this is my best friend, Marlowe."

Claire was walking over to meet Marlowe, but Isaac beat her to it.

"Hey, I'm Isaac," he said, extending his hand. "Beau's younger, more charismatic brother."

"Nice to meet you," Marlowe said with a coy smile.

Beau and I exchanged a look. I suspected Isaac

and Marlowe would be spending some time alone in the future, possibly between the sheets.

I wondered if it would be before or after he found out Marlowe broadcasted the details of her sexcapades for the world to listen to.

Either way, I wasn't going to be the one to tell him.

Beau

"I'M ON MY WAY," I mumbled, groaning from the pain in my ribs when I rolled over in bed and got up.

In the week Charlie had been home, Shelby and I had developed a Pavlovian response to his cries. He wailed, one of us ran. Sometimes both. Whether it was two in the afternoon or two in the morning, we were on call to meet his needs.

When I got to the nursery Shelby had put together for him in the guest room of her apartment and found his crib empty, I panicked. He was crying, but he wasn't in his crib?

"Babe?" I called as I walked toward the living room.

"We're in here."

When I walked into the living room, she was sitting in the recliner with him, looking soft and sweet with her hair down and her glasses on. I squinted at the clock on the wall, then did a double take.

"One fifteen? How is that possible? It should be dark outside."

Shelby smiled at me. "It's one fifteen p.m. Your parents came by early this morning and I gave them the milk I pumped and they took him to their house for a while. I slept for six incredible, uninterrupted hours."

I scratched my head. "I remember getting up with him at three something. Have I been asleep since then?"

"Yep. I knew you needed to get some rest."

She was always thinking of me, even the little things. Not that sleep was little by any means these days. But in addition to letting me get some uninterrupted rest, she'd had my favorite coffee delivered to her place and upgraded her cable package so I could watch hockey games. I loved that she didn't even mention those things, because she didn't seek acknowledgment. She just quietly cared for both me and Charlie.

I went over to her and reached for our son. "Not

as much as you need it. I've got him now. Go lie down."

"No, I'm good. Your mom brought over a casserole and I think I'm going to pop it in the oven. Are you hungry?"

"Starving."

She passed Charlie to me, his arms shooting into the air with alarm. He was the sweetest baby I'd ever seen, and Shelby and I were both smitten with him.

"Marlowe said she'll stay with him tomorrow morning so we can attend the funerals," she said as she walked into the kitchen.

"Okay, good."

Tomorrow was the first day of the many funerals for those killed in the arena explosions. The fire investigators knew two bombs had been remotely detonated, one in a storage room and another in a boiler room. Whoever had done it either had access to nearly all of the arena, or they'd found a way to bypass not having access. The investigations were going to take a while.

Whatever they discovered, it couldn't bring back the twenty-two people who had been killed. Five of them were my teammates, fifteen others worked for the Coyotes' organization, and two were fans buying tickets.

It was lucky more people hadn't been killed.

There were seven people who were still in critical condition, and if they made it, their lives would never be the same. Andie had lost her leg below the knee to amputation, because it couldn't be saved, and one of the maintenance guys had lost both of his legs.

The arena would have to be torn down when the investigation was finished, and Mila had called the rest of our season off. There was no way any of us could have played. Many of us were recovering from physical injuries, and we all had grief to work through.

"I need to get to Dalton's funeral early. I'm a pallbearer," I said. "Can't remember if I told you that or not."

"You didn't." Shelby approached me from behind and put her arms around me. "Do you need to go home and get a suit this afternoon?"

"I asked Isaac to bring me some stuff; he's coming by this evening."

"Oh, good."

"He wouldn't be sorry if Marlowe was here when he dropped by."

I felt her chuckle against my back, her cheek resting against it. "Oh really? He said that?"

"Should I just call Marlowe and tell her what he said? Save you the trouble of relaying it?"

She gave me a playful smack and went back into the kitchen. "No. Tell me everything."

Charlie made a little cooing sound, his mouth making an O shape and his eyes rounding like something surprised him.

"Babe, hurry. We need a picture of this."

Shelby rushed in with her phone, but she wasn't fast enough to capture a photo.

"I think we might have the cutest baby ever created," I said, leaning down to talk to Charlie in a soft tone. "You're even cute when you're shitting yourself, aren't you?"

"Speaking of," Shelby said, walking back into the kitchen, "he probably needs a diaper change."

"On my way."

"Wait!" She stuck her head out from around the corner of the kitchen. "What did Isaac say about Marlowe?"

"When he texted me that he'd bring my stuff by, he asked if Marlowe would be here. I said I didn't know, and that was it."

"So obviously he's interested."

I shrugged. "Sounds like it to me."

"Okay. I'm putting the casserole in and then taking a shower."

"Ten-four."

I carried Charlie into his nursery and put him on

the changing table, taking out a fresh diaper and his wipes. At first, I'd been slow and methodical with diaper changes, because Asher had made the rookie mistake of not putting the diapers on right with Anderson and he'd peed through them in his sleep. I wanted to get it right, because sleep was too precious to lose over poor diaper technique.

The first time Charlie peed on my face while I was slowly changing his diaper was the last. Since then, I'd cut my diapering time in half. My siblings were never going to let me forget it. I wasn't sure why I'd even told them about it in our group chat.

"Got to keep the family jewels clean," I said as I cleaned Charlie with a wipe. "I know it's cold, little dude, but I'll try to go fast."

Dalton had a son. He was only two years old, and now his father was gone. I remembered the picture Dalton sent out to the entire team of his baby boy in the tiny Coyotes sweater we'd sent as a gift right after he was born.

"Life is too short sometimes," I told Charlie. "And sometimes it's not fair. Sometimes we get a raw deal. That's why we have to laugh as often as we can and love as hard as we can. Let's promise each other that, okay?"

After fastening his diaper, I gently folded his little fingers into a fist for a fist bump. I couldn't believe how much I already loved my son. I was so damn lucky Shelby felt the same connection between us that I did. Our little family of three had quickly become my world.

"Obviously, we're putting you in this one," I said, picking up a hockey-stick-covered onesie from the folded stack on the shelf of the changing table. "We'll have you in your first pair of skates in no time."

Once he was dressed, I picked him up, holding him against my chest as I left the room. He was starting to fuss, so I opened the door to the bathroom and spoke through the crack.

"Hey babe, you think he might be hungry?"

"Probably," Shelby said from the shower. "And a ridiculous amount of milk is leaking out of me right now. Just use some formula. I can't pump enough to keep up with him and I really need this shower."

"Okay."

"Hey, buddy, it's all good," I told Charlie. "We're going to do something really fun and then you get a bottle, okay?"

My pulse raced as I walked into the kitchen and opened the second can of powdered baby formula I'd asked Fiona to sneak over to me. The only one Shelby knew about was hidden in a cabinet.

Rocking Charlie with one arm, I used my free hand to drop something into the powder, then I pushed it beneath the surface an inch or so with my finger.

"It's like a treasure hunt," I told Charlie. "Those are fun, little man."

I put Charlie in his swing and turned on the lights and music of his mobile, which always held his attention. He immediately quieted, transfixed by the spinning light above him. Then I went back to the bathroom and opened the door, speaking into the crack again.

"Babe?"

"Yeah?"

"Um, we might have a problem."

Immediately, I heard her turn off the shower. "What?"

"You should come look at the powdered formula you ordered. I found a rock in it."

"What? Oh my god, what!?"

She ran from the bathroom, clutching a towel to her front and trailing water everywhere. I was taking advantage of her type *A* nature, but it was for a good reason.

"If there's a rock in there, I will sue the shit out of that company," she ranted, ripping the lid off the can and digging through it. "Like it's not hard enough for new mothers to trust what they're putting into their babies' bodies, that is completely unacc"

She pulled out the two-carat solitaire set in a platinum band I'd bought when she was thirty-four weeks along. I knew for sure I wanted her to be my wife, and I wanted the proposal to be spontaneous.

Today felt right. When Shelby accompanied me to the funerals for my teammates, the Coyotes staff, and fans who had died in the explosions, I wanted her to have this ring on her finger. It was my promise to her, and to Charlie.

When she looked from the ring back to me, I was down on one knee.

"Shelby Grant, I love you more deeply than words can convey. You and Charlie are everything to me. Will you be my wife?"

She smiled through the tears running down her cheeks. "Beau! Oh my god, Beau. I'm naked and soaking wet and...wow. I didn't expect this. I'm just..."

"Babe? Are you not sure?"

Had I fucked it up? Should I have gone with a rose-covered rooftop garden and a thousand candles?

"Yes! I mean, yes! Of course I'll marry you."

I stood and swept her into my arms, her wet hair soaking through my shirt when I kissed her.

"You just made me the happiest man in the world," I said.

"We're getting married!" She put her palms on my cheeks, glowing with happiness. "I love you so much."

"I love you, too."

She wrinkled her nose, still grinning. "Good, because I'm pretty sure there's breast milk soaking through this towel onto whatever you're wearing."

I set her down and tugged at the towel, eager to get a look at her enlarged breasts, which were easily double *D*s for now.

"Jesus, those are sexy," I murmured.

She squealed and pulled the towel against her stomach. "I'm leaking milk. That's definitely not hot."

"Bullshit." I looked down at my crotch, my erection outlined against my gym shorts.

"Five more weeks," she reminded me.

"I slipped the doctor a Benjamin and he said you're cleared for sex in two weeks."

She laughed, trying to wrap the towel around herself. "Yeah, good one."

She tucked the towel around her so it was secure, then slid the ring onto her finger.

"Let's go show Charlie," she said.

When we got into the living room, he was kicking his legs, still staring at the spinning lights.

"Look, lovey," Shelby said, leaning down to show

him her sparkling ring. "Mommy and Daddy are getting married."

She turned off the swing and he immediately started fussing again. She ran a hand over his hair as she picked him up, walking over to the recliner.

"You can eat, and then we'll celebrate," she said. "Sound good?"

As I watched her feed our son, I was already celebrating inside. I wasn't sure hockey would ever be the same for me after the devastation caused by the explosion, but I knew one thing for sure.

I had an incredible family to lean on during the hard times, and I'd never let them down. My forever had found me at Mountain Top with a binder and a mission, and I was damn glad she did.

EPILOGUE

Six months later

Beau

"HEY, CHECK OUT MY KID." I turned my phone to show Charlie's toothless grin to Coach.

"Cute. He looks like you."

Coach's hair had gone from salt and pepper to almost fully gray in the past six months. Though we were practicing at a college arena, things were still unsettled for our team, and they would be for a while.

"If everyone could take a seat, I'd like to get started," Mila said.

We were meeting in a conference room on the college campus Mila was renting rink time and office space from. It wasn't ideal. The office space was spread out over campus and we had to share the rink with the college team, but at least we were in the same area. For the first couple of months after the arena was destroyed, things were a mess.

There were so many unanswered questions, but the most important thing had been recovering the bodies from the rubble and burying those we'd lost.

As the acting team captain, I was included in weekly meetings with the Coyotes' top brass. I held a weekly meeting with my teammates after that to let them know what was going on.

Frankly, our weekly get-togethers had quickly come to mean more to us than just a briefing on the efforts to rebuild our team and arena. We met up at local restaurants or a teammate's home and talked a little bit of hockey and a whole lot of life.

We'd lost five of our twenty-three players that day. No warning. Not only was there a hole in our team that could never be filled, but many of us were dealing with survivor's guilt and reliving the trauma of that day. Petty disagreements had been forgotten. We were bonded for life now, and everyone knew the only way we'd get through this new hell was together.

"I have great news for the first time in a while," Mila said as she took her seat at the head of the conference table.

She looked at her assistant Dave, who stood next to the doorway of the conference room. "Bring him in, please."

Dave opened the door to the conference room and waved someone in. I was floored when Ford Barrett walked into the room, his expression all business.

"Meet the newest member of the Coyotes family," Mila said.

This was a top-level administration meeting between eight of the team's top executives, coaches, and me. I could tell from the shocked looks on several faces around the table that I wasn't the only one who was just finding out about this.

"Hey, man," I said, standing up and approaching Ford with a grin. "I'm so stoked you're here. Welcome."

He gave me a slight smile and nodded. Ford was one of the highest-ranked offensive players in the league. Everyone had been sure his next contract would be with New York. I knew Mila had paid dearly to acquire him for our team. The Ice Queen had her flaws, but her commitment to this team was rock solid. All of us had grown to appreciate her more in the past six months. She'd really stepped up and made a huge effort to take care of every family who lost a loved one in the explosions.

Ford went around the table and shook hands, everyone standing up to greet him enthusiastically. Mila was right—this was the first great news our team had gotten in a while.

Ford wasn't just a superstar athlete. He was also known to be a strong leader with a level head and a relentless drive to win. He'd been the captain of his last team, the Minnesota Mammoths. He was a shoo-in to become captain of the Coyotes.

I'd reluctantly agreed to be the acting captain, but I didn't want the role permanently. Life had changed a lot since Shelby and I had Charlie, and when things got back to normal and I was traveling for hockey again, I wanted to be with my family as much as possible.

"Have a seat, Ford," Mila said, gesturing at the open seat next to mine.

He sat down, immediately reaching for the pitcher of water in the middle of the table and pouring a glass.

"An announcement about Ford's signing will be made tonight," Mila said. "He'll start practicing with the team tomorrow morning."

There were smiles and nods of appreciation.

Though we didn't have our own arena and we were still trying to find a new groove as a team, this would absolutely provide the guys with a boost. Ford would join me and Colby on the first line, and I was excited to see what the three of us could do together.

There was no way to replace Dalton, but he would have wanted us to move forward and win.

"Unfortunately, I don't have anything new to report on property acquisition for the new arena," Mila said. "Even when I bid on the parcels we need through shell corporations, it gets traced back to me and the price gets jacked up to triple the market value. I think we're going to have to work with the local government to pursue eminent domain. It's not the way I wanted to go, and it's going to be a political shit show. The governor is no fan of mine so he'll be putting up roadblocks left and right."

"Our temp arena seats are selling like crazy," the Coyotes business manager, Jane, said. "So we know that won't be an issue."

Mila scoffed. "Yeah, we can't have a single open seat in the temp arena. Tell the people in the sales department to keep those season tickets moving."

"The temp arena is a massive reduction in capacity, though," Jane said. "One-third as many seats. And as you know, we reduced ticket prices because of the inconveniences to fans like less parking and fewer concessions."

Mila nodded. "Some of the city officials are digging in their heels about wanting us to repurpose an old space, but that's not going to work. I'm holding firm on a new venue, and I want financial support from the city."

"This bullshit doesn't help any," Coach said, tossing a copy of the local newspaper, the *Denver Chronicle*, on the table. "Did you see Shea Lawrence's column this morning?"

Mila narrowed her eyes. "That viper is at the top of my shit list. I'm sick of her rants about how violent hockey is, and if she thinks taxpayers haven't supported every major pro sports venue in this country, she's out of her mind."

"Maybe we need a full-court press marketing campaign about building a new arena," the team's CFO Brian said. "We could hire some consultants to put together economic impact numbers and schedule meetings with business owners in the area to get some traction."

Mila nodded. "That's a great idea. And it'll help with our eminent domain case, too."

I unlocked my phone and pulled up my newest picture of Charlie, the one I'd taken this morning and shown Coach.

"That's my son," I whispered to Ford, showing him my screen.

He nodded but didn't even crack a smile. I didn't take it personally; he had a reputation for being on the serious side.

Mila covered a few more things pertaining to the business office, but I was zoned out. Shelby and I were getting married in a small ceremony at my parents' house next month, and I had to decide what beers we were having. It was pretty much the only thing Shelby, my mom, and Fiona were letting me decide, but I was rolling with it. As long as we ended up married, the details weren't important to me.

Finally, Mila dismissed the meeting. I was going to suggest Ford be selected as our new team captain at tomorrow night's team gathering, and I hoped this would be my final weekly administrative meeting.

Ford stood and I clapped him on the back. "Let me know if there's anything you need. I can put you in touch with a realtor, banker, or anything else you might want."

"Thanks," he said, his brow pulled down in a permanent frown. "I'm just going to get an apartment for now."

"Well, we've got a team meeting tomorrow night at Dominic Locke's house at seven. I'll text you the address."

He nodded. "I'll be there."

I was about to walk away when he opened his mouth to say something else.

"Hey, Beau."

"Yeah?"

"I know I'm coming into a tough situation. Meaning tough for the guys who were here that day and lost teammates. Not tough for me. I don't want to step on any toes, and I'd appreciate it if you could watch my back and let me know if I make any missteps."

"Absolutely. I appreciate you saying that."

He smiled, his jaw set and his gaze determined. "I chose to come here because I want to be part of your comeback. Let's make this the season we show everyone what this team is made of."

There was a lump in my throat as I responded.

"Hell yeah. Let's do it."

Up next in the Colorado Coyotes series is Ford and Shea's story, The Opponent, releasing May 30, 2023. Preorder it HERE.

ALSO BY BRENDA ROTHERT

CHICAGO BLAZE SERIES

Book 1 - Anton

Book 2 - Luca

Book 3 - Victor

Book 4 - Knox

Book 5 - Alexei

Book 6 - Easy

Book 7 - Jonah

Book 8 - Kit

Book 9 - Olivier

SIN CITY SAINTS SERIES

Book 1 - Maverick

Book 2 - Pike

Book 3 - Pax

ST. LOUS MAVERICKS SERIES

Book 1 - Hard Fall

Book 2 - Hard Limit

Book 3 - Hard Pass

Buried

Sweet Sixteen

His

Alpha Mail

Healing Touch

Barely Breathing

Exiled

ABOUT THE AUTHOR

Brenda Rothert lives in Central Illinois with her husband, children and two dogs. She loves to hear from readers through her website or her Facebook Group, Rothert's Readers.

www.ingramcontent.com/pod-product-compliance
Lightning Source LLC
Chambersburg PA
CBHW011852300726
48970CB00009B/2753